SKY THERAPY

A STORY ABOUT TWO PEOPLE TRYING NOT TO FALL IN LOVE

MARINA PACHECO

MARINA PACHECO

Sign up for Marina Pacheco's no-spam newsletter that only goes out when there is a new book or freebie available and get my free collection of short stories!

Details can be found at the end of this book.

CONTENTS

1

‘**J**AQ!’

The call rang out across the pub and she homed in on Sarah, waving from amongst a huddle of work colleagues.

Jaq threaded her way through the dense Thursday evening crowd, already regretting saying yes to this invitation. She'd been bemoaning her single state via text a few nights ago to Sarah, who was about to get married.

Come to my work engagement party, she'd messaged. *We have loads of nice looking single men.*

She would know. She was marrying someone she worked with. Seeing her best friend marry made Jaq feel like she was missing out.

One by one, everyone she knew at school had got hitched. But as long as Sarah had remained single, she'd been okay. Now she was the last in their friends' group.

She wasn't usually influenced by social pressure, but she'd kicked into overdrive on this one. It proved her desperation that she'd agreed to go to this party and now it was too late to back out.

'Guys, this is Jaq, my best friend since primary school, and soon to be my maid-of-honour.'

'Hi,' Jaq said and waved to encompass the large gathering.

As to be expected from a marketing agency, they all looked trendy, half on the artistic side with colourful hair, tattoos and piercings, the other half in sharp suits, although they had all loosened their ties. They'd taken over an and area that included a booth where the artistic people had settled. The rest huddled around Sarah, who reeled off their names.

'Don't worry if you can't remember them,' a friendly woman with a nose piercing, who'd been introduced as Liz, said. 'There's far too many of us. I'm terrible with names as it is. I'll probably have forgotten yours within the next five minutes.'

'I think we all have that problem,' Jaq said, although for her it was a lie.

As a police officer, a detective in the serious crimes squad, she never forgot a name. Not that she was going to mention that, or her job. It put people off, especially prospective boyfriends.

'Here, sit beside me.' Liz squidged up along the frayed red velvet bench, forcing the man beside her to do the same. 'This is Simon. He's the best designer in our team, and going to stand in for Sarah while she's on honeymoon.'

Simon gave her a polite, but not very interested, smile. That was okay. She'd already dismissed him as a potential boyfriend. He was good looking, dark eyes, long eyelashes, a mop of slightly overlong, wavy brown hair, but thin, far too thin.

That either made him one of those men who was an obsessive runner or gay. In her experience, gay men were as fixated as women on their weight. This was further reinforced by the fact that he was nursing his pint. He was only a third of the way through, with another two pints lined up beside it, while the rest of the party were knocking their drinks back in style.

And another thing, it was hot in the pub, yet Simon was wearing a long-sleeved t-shirt. Only people with scars on their arms did that when everyone else had their sleeves rolled up and were dabbing at flushed, overheated faces.

In her line of work, Jaq had come across a lot of drug addicts. They were classic long sleeve wearers. That might not have been Simon's issue, but it was another mark against him. She wanted someone law abiding, someone who had always been law-abiding.

She had her standards, after all, even if she was desperate. And it was a strength to be able to cut people out immediately. After all, she didn't have time to waste. Her work was too demanding to be distracted by an angsty love.

She needed something clean and simple, someone who could support her as she would support them, somebody with whom she could have a meeting of minds. Somebody handsome that she could show off at parties would be a pleasant bonus.

'So tell me, Jaq,' Liz said, using that technique of repeating a person's name to remember it. 'What line of work are you in?'

Damn, straight off the bat. Jaq had her stock answer, though.

'I'm a civil servant.'

'What does that even mean?' Simon said, much to Jaq's surprise.

People rarely bothered with a followup question. Civil servant sounded so boring most people just changed the subject.

'You could be anything from a nurse to a Whitehall Mandarin,' Simon continued, like an interrogator who wasn't about to let anybody off the hook.

'Nothing as exciting as a Whitehall Mandarin. Although I wouldn't mind their salary.'

'Wouldn't we all?' Liz said with a laugh.

Jaq used that to break eye contact with the too inquisitive Simon and change the direction of the conversation to Sarah's wedding. Liz was happy to go along with that. She launched into how surprised she was that Sarah was marrying Aaron, who was in Sales. Jaq gathered from the friendly ribbing that the people in Sales were a different tribe. They were the suit wearing contingent of this group, and a not altogether popular one.

Aaron, though, was well liked. A crowd surrounded him as he regaled them with a story of how he messed up a drop kick in his latest rugby match. Sarah was clinging to his arm, laughing, which brought on a wave of irritated jealousy in Jaq.

Aaron was a great catch: tall, well built, blond, outgoing and earned plenty of money. Jaq was losing her best friend to that great hunk of muscle. Still, he was friendly enough, and she'd be able to relegate him to husband status and not have to see him very much once they were married.

Jaq took her pint glass, murmured something about catching up with Sarah and hurried back to her side.

'So, how do I tell the singletons from the rest?' Jaq said into Sarah's ear.

In her experience, not having a wedding ring was no indicator. Sarah looked around, weighing up the crowd.

'I'll introduce you. Don't bother with those three for a start,' she said, pointing discreetly to three men, one so obviously camp he had to be gay, another rather nice looking Asian guy and Simon.

'All gay?'

'The first two, yes. Simon,' Sarah shrugged. 'Nobody knows.'

That was such a strange comment that it piqued Jaq's curiosity.

'What do you mean?'

'He doesn't seem interested in anyone, men or women. We all like him, and he will chat with whoever's around. He's also a hard worker and chips in on projects if we need him, but he keeps to himself.'

Jaq stepped sideways to give herself some room as she was constantly being jabbed in the back by some woman's handbag.

'Keeps to himself? In what way?'

Jaq's detective instincts always kicked in when she heard about oddballs. It made her wonder what they were up to.

'Never having a partner, I guess, or interested in having one,' Sarah said as she took a meditative sip of her beer and stared at Simon, currently chatting to a young blond guy with green highlights on the other side of Liz.

'And he socialises but only to a point. He's always one of the first to leave. He'll buy a round of drinks and then go, without touching all the pints that have stacked up before him.

'We call it the Simon bonus. We just share his lot out with whoever's still around. He's the same at work. He leaves on time. I don't think he's ever been the last out of the office.

'And he doesn't like one-to-ones. He'll go out in a group, but if it dwindles, he leaves. I've never once seen him having lunch with just one other person. It's a group or not at all.'

'Huh, that is unusual.' But since Jaq couldn't find a criminal angle for that kind of behaviour, she lost interest. 'Okay, so show me the best of what's still available.'

'Artistic or materialistic?' Sarah said with a laugh as she waved a hand that encompassed the crowd.

'What difference does it make?' Jaq asked, but gave it some consideration as she looked Aaron up and down.

He was very well built, and good looking. His colleagues were similar, men who spent lunchtime at the gym. All with short crew cuts and their subtle signs of wealth, such as the name brand watches and the darker guy with the gold signet ring.

'I always thought I'd go for someone artistic like me,' Sarah said as Aaron slipped his arm around her waist while still chatting with his mates. 'But the sales guys earn commission, so while they have the same basic salary, they can more than double it in a good month.'

'I didn't know you were so materialistic,' Jaq said, well aware that Sarah wasn't attracted by the money.

'Love at first sight,' Sarah said as she leaned up and gave Aaron a peck on his cheek.

He turned around and gave her a much longer kiss on the lips that made all his male friends give a roar, half of approval, half a demand to stop. Jaq sympathised. It was cringy to watch such a loved up couple.

'Talk to Rob,' Aaron said, grinning at Jaq over Sarah's shoulder. 'He said you looked fit.'

It didn't thrill Jaq to hear she'd been a part of the men's conversation, but she supposed it was fair enough if they were also looking to meet someone.

'Him,' Sarah said as she pointed to the man with the signet ring.

She also rolled her eyes, a warning to Jaq, but as Rob was making his way towards them, Jaq closed the gap, and said, 'Fancy getting some air?'

'Do you smoke?' he asked as he took a pack of cigarettes out of his pocket and started pushing his way through the crowd towards the doors.

'I don't,' Jaq said, as they got outside and joined the people standing about, pint in one hand, cigarette in the other.

Since the indoor smoking ban had come into force, the smokers were now relegated to huddling outside. Fine on a comfortable spring day, but not great throughout the wet and windy winter.

'I started when I was thirteen,' Rob said, flicking the bottom of his pack till a cigarette rose sufficiently to grab it between his lips. 'If there was one thing I could tell myself if I went back in time, it would be to leave the cigs alone.'

'So you've tried to give up?'

Jaq's father was a smoker, so she was used to it, although she would have preferred that a potential life partner not be a smoker.

'Hundreds of times,' Rob said, and Jaq decided he had a nice voice, despite the cockney twang.

Maybe this evening hadn't been a complete waste of time after all.

Simon stepped out of the pub with a sense of relief. Liz was getting a little too friendly the drunker she got. It made things awkward.

Sarah's friend, maid-of-honour or whatever, was also odd. She was attractive, straight brown hair tied back off her face but with a fringe that framed and softened the look that was Japanese in style. And she was fit. There were toned muscles under her draped grey dress. But the way she looked at him was unsettling.

It felt like she was seeing too much, reminiscent of the police. That brought up all sorts of memories he tried to keep buried. Now he looked around. Time to go home, but which was the best route?

Walk across Tower Bridge and then to the Docklands Light Rail, he decided, after a moment's reflection. The whole route was plastered with CCTV because up to the Docklands it was a prime area for socialising and tourists. If nothing else, the London Mayor was keen to keep tourists safe.

Simon had bought his flat with two criteria: proximity to public transport and crime levels. The online crime map was a really useful tool for working out the safest places to live.

His flat had a low crime rating thanks to two factors. One, the high numbers of CCTV cameras lining the surrounding roads. Two, the large police station three blocks away. Criminals avoided police stations. There were far too many officers frequenting the local shops, pubs and cafes or just roaming about.

It suited Simon, though, because he had to be careful about everything. About where he lived, about what he did and how he interacted with people. His history meant certain jobs were entirely out of the question, no teaching jobs, no customer facing jobs, no job where he might land up alone with one other person.

Fortunately, he was good at art, and a charity had got him access to a design course. So an open plan office job at a large advertising agency was a good fit. But even there he kept his distance, which extended to turning down an offer of promotion to manager.

He wasn't good with people. That was one reason. He also struggled to read and managers had a lot more paperwork, although he probably could have found a workaround for that. The clincher was that managers had one-to-one meetings with their staff and he wasn't willing to risk that.

Now, as Simon set off into the twilight, he took a deep breath of cool air. He enjoyed walking. Maybe because he'd been a prisoner in his own home until the age of fourteen. The walk across Tower Bridge, with the stiff wind blowing down the Thames, blew out all his stress.

It was always a superb view and out of habit, he stopped at the midpoint of the bridge and looked downriver. The Thames was a deep, rippling green with a pale blue line where it met the sky. Above that, the sky was tending towards inky with regular dabs of almost translucent fluffy clouds picked out in a burnt orange as the last rays of the sun hit them. It was too dark to take a photo, but he committed the range of colours to memory.

He liked the sky. It was big and wide and open and it brought peace with it. He never tired of looking up, and spent much of his free time painting the sky in all its wide variety.

He took a final deep, satisfied breath and carried on to catch his train. It was just a single line and ten stops before he got home. Then a walk along a well lit, heavily surveilled road to his flat.

He lived on the top floor, deliberately, because he got better views of the sky from up there. The building was old though and didn't have a lift. When he was tired like today and drained from having to interact with people, the four stories seemed exhausting.

Once through his front door, his motion sensitive automatic recording system kicked in. He checked it to make sure nobody had come in while he was away. Nobody ever had, but it was best to be careful. Nobody, aside from him, had ever been in the flat. He'd even had it decorated before moving in so that he wouldn't have to share the space with anybody else.

Simon made himself a cup of tea, adding in his usual two lumps of crystallised ginger and settled on his sofa with a sigh of relief. It was good to be home. He took a first tentative sip while he examined his latest, nearly complete, cloud painting on the easel across the room, mentally filling in what still had to be done: mostly highlights to the fluffy edges of the clouds.

His mind drifted on, thinking about the work gathering, and Liz, who'd been extra chatty. He quite liked her as a colleague. She had a clean, no nonsense drawing style that was well suited to advertising.

Then he considered that woman. It took him a moment to recall her name, but it finally came to him, Jaq. Maybe it was because it was a strange name for a woman that it had stuck.

The other option was that he was attracted to her. That made him nervous. But he was human, after all, and in his thirties, so it was normal to be attracted to a woman. He had to keep reminding himself of that.

Being fascinated by a woman wasn't an unhealthy perversion. All the same, it was just as well he wouldn't be seeing her again. It was best to steer clear of any temptation that left him in a turmoil of desire and equally powerful nauseous revulsion.

2

— · —

'ALL RIGHT PEOPLE,' DETECTIVE Chief Inspector Morris shouted over the hubbub of the office. 'We have a missing person.'

'Oh great,' Jaq said as she put down the bag that she'd been shoving her glasses and phone into before heading home. 'It always happens at the end of the day on the weekend shift.'

'This is Elizabeth Chadwick,' DCI Morris said, swiping left on the smart board so that a large photo of a woman with a pierced nose appeared. 'She has been missing for 38 hours. Uniforms haven't been able to find her, so they've handed everything over to us. We've got some catching up to do. Divide into your usual three teams.'

The unit swung into well-oiled action as each team took over a particular section of the search.

'Our usual, friends and known associates,' Darren Jones, Jaq's senior partner, said as the two of them opened the case file on their computers. 'But let's catch up on all the details first.'

'Elizabeth Chadwick?' Jaq examined the photograph and personal details of the missing woman again. 'She looks familiar.'

'Do you know her, Burnham?'

Darren was a damn good detective and might have been her ideal life partner from that point of view, though sadly, happily married. Besides, too old and not her physical type. Hating herself for it, Jaq couldn't get past the extensive acne scaring, the wonky nose, and the almost translucent ginger hair that he kept to a short buzz cut.

Jaq scanned the missing person's information again and spotted the place of work, London Marketing.

'Of course!' she said, snapping her fingers. 'Liz.'

'So you do know her.'

'I met her on Thursday at a pub. She's a colleague of Sarah's.'

'Ah. Not too close of a connection that you'd have to be off the case, but make sure to put it in the case notes.'

'Shit,' Jaq said and shook her head. 'She seemed like a nice woman.'

'Let's hope we find her then.' Darren swiped through the pages of information the uniformed police had already gathered. 'It's 38 hours since she disappeared. That's not good. Her mother reported her missing. They live together and Liz went out on Saturday evening to see her boyfriend but didn't turn up. Team one will be looking more thoroughly into him. Her mother only realised that she wasn't home when she got up on this morning. Uniforms have already checked all the hospitals between the pub and home. CCTV, though, shows her coming this way.'

'This way?' Jaq scanned the document until she got to the same place as him. 'Towards our station? Do you think she was being followed?'

'It doesn't look like it on the CCTV. But if she felt like she was being followed, then heading towards a police station is a good move. And we know some stalkers are really good at avoiding cameras.'

'Yeah.'

Jaq worked her way through the rest of the information, friend and family contacts. This would involve more door-to-door questioning, although local constables had already started on that and handed over copies of their notes. After looking through those, Jaq consulted their lists of known local offenders and colleagues' addresses. 'Oh, look here,' she said a couple of hours later, tapping an address on the screen. 'That's Jasmine Road too, really close to where Liz was last seen.'

'And who is it?'

'One of her colleagues. Simon White. I met him on Thursday too. He's a bit odd.'

'Odd how?' Darren said, his fingers already tapping through his tablet, calling up the crime database for information on Simon White.

'Nothing I could put my finger on exactly.'

'A bit of a creep?'

'More like... hyper vigilant, not willing to just let things drop. He was also sitting next to Liz on Thursday, although he left a couple of hours before the party ended.'

'Worth a visit,' Darren said, and slipped his tablet into his work bag. 'Nothing comes up about him on an initial search, but it's worth checking out for now.'

'Yeah, let's go. I'll notify the team, who will be questioning the rest of the work colleagues, so we don't duplicate. I'll get Amber to dig deeper into this Simon White in the meantime.'

The doorbell shocked Simon into wakefulness and he realised he'd dozed off. His iPad was lying on the dining table, the show he was watching still running. He reached to press pause, his hand shaking, as the doorbell rang again.

His already pounding heart lurched as he noted it was nine pm. It was far too late for a delivery, especially on a Sunday. Not that he was expecting one, but deliveries were the only reason for anybody to be at his door.

The bell sounded again, insistent, buzzing one, two, three times. Maybe there was a fire. But the smoke detectors–

The bell again. He hurried to the door. He should have checked the answerphone, but he was so thrown by being rushed that he just wrenched the door open.

His breath caught. Police! Two plainclothes cops in the front, two in uniforms standing behind them.

'Simon White?' the female officer asked. 'I'm Detective Inspector Burnham, Violent Crimes Squad,' she said, flashing her badge.

She waved her warrant card too quickly for him to read it. Not that his brain could process anything. Weirdly enough, she seemed familiar, although Simon couldn't think why.

'Yes?'

He could barely speak. His heart rate surged, and he clutched the side of the door tighter to prevent his hand from shaking.

'We'd like to ask you a few questions, if that's alright, sir?'

'A... about what?'

'Mr White, you know Elizabeth Chadwick, don't you?'

'Liz?' Simon was trying to understand and to get himself under control. 'What's happened to Liz?'

'Why would anything happen to Ms Chadwick?' the male officer said, a big bruiser of a man with the off kilter nose of a boxer.

'Why else would you be here?' Simon said with difficulty, because his mouth had dried up.

'I'm afraid Ms Chadwick has disappeared–'

The female detective's lips kept moving and Simon knew she was still speaking, but he couldn't take it in. Dear God, what was happening?

'– so we'd appreciate it if you'd let us in to check your house.'

Simon blinked at her, on the verge of panic but trying not to show it. She smiled back, a blank, professional, we're waiting, kind of smile.

'I know you,' he muttered, trying to drag his fragmented mind back into order.

'Yes, I'm D.I. Jaq Burnham,' she said, emphasising the Jaq. 'We met at Sarah's engagement party. Now, will you let us take a look around, or will I need to get a warrant?'

Simon hesitated for a split second, but Liz was missing and he'd do whatever it took to help the police find her. So he stepped to the left, pulling the door open as he did and waved them in.

'Thank you,' D.I. Burnham said, and the detectives stepped inside while the uniforms took up position on either side of his door. 'While we're looking, would you mind answering a few questions?'

This wasn't the first time in his life that police had arrived at Simon's home, although the last time he'd been a lot younger, in his father's house, and he'd hidden away as they'd stormed in. Weirdly, even though this was a lot more low key, it felt as traumatic.

Still, he did as ordered. Now that they were here, his best bet, and Liz's, was to get this over with as quickly as possible.

'Can you tell me, please, when was the last time you saw Ms Chadwick?'

'Thursday night, at the party.' Simon glanced out of his front door to the balcony that ran the length of the block of flats. Neighbours had appeared, some peeking through a crack in their front door, others more blatantly standing outside, watching the show.

'You haven't seen her since?' DI Burnham said as she crooked her finger to indicate he should follow her into the flat.

'No. I haven't seen her.'

Her partner, in the meantime, had headed to his closed bedroom door.

'What is this room?' he asked.

'Bedroom,' Simon said.

'Would you open the door for us please, sir?' the man said.

It felt to Simon like a worse intrusion being asked to open his house himself, like a victim slapping his own face. But he did as asked and pushed open the door.

'What about you?' Burnham carried on, as Simon stood aside to let the big cop enter his room. 'What did you do after you left the party?'

'I came straight home.'

'Can anybody corroborate that?' Burnham said as she took a pair of bright blue latex gloves out of a sealed pack and pulled them on.

'I have a home security system,' Simon barely managed to whisper. This was getting worse and worse. 'It will have time stamps.'

'A home security system?' D.I. Burnham paused, the second latex glove only half on. She looked like she thought this was a distinctly odd thing to have. 'How about the rest of the weekend?'

'I've been home.'

'All weekend?'

'Yes.'

'You never went out.'

'No.'

'Alright, please open this door for me too,' Burnham said, indicating the bathroom.

Simon did as ordered and tried to pull himself together at the same time. He'd been so shocked he'd done everything so far without thinking. But now he was regretting his capitulation.

He belatedly remembered the advice Rat Face had given everyone at the young offender's institution. Rat Face because he had a rather prominent set of front teeth, although Simon had always thought he looked more like a mouse with his big, round glasses. He'd been the local genius because, unlike most of them, he could read and write really well and spent his life with his nose in a book.

He'd always told them that whether they were innocent or guilty, they should say as little as possible to the police and block whatever they were trying to do.

'Because they'll just try to fit you up. They decide who's guilty first, and then they find the evidence that proves it. Or they plant it,' he'd added ominously.

'Thank you for your co-operation. Now please wait out here with these officers,' Burnham said, pointing at two uniforms.

Simon blinked at her, realising he'd zoned out. She waited till he nodded agreement before she went in for a closer examination of his bathroom. It was too late for him to stop her. So, against everything Rat Face had warned him about, he remained in the doorway, watching, just in case they tried to plant something on him.

Jaq was struck by the thought that Simon White was more nervous than most. He'd turned white as a sheet when he'd seen cops at his door, but that was to be expected. It was rarely a good sign for anyone.

But he had yet to calm down. His tightly clasped hands were shaking, and he looked unfocused. He looked so petrified he couldn't even concentrate as his eyes darted from her to Darren and back again.

'Any luck?' Darren asked as Jaq went back to digging through the laundry basket.

Jaq shook her head.

'Have you found his security system?'

'Yeah, it's hooked up to his computer. We'll see if we can take his computer with us. Aside from that, no woman, but I suppose that was too much to ask for. No signs of anybody at all or a struggle. The place is immaculate.'

That was true, Jaq thought, as her gaze swept over a modern, open plan flat. A kitchen ran along the right-hand side wall to halfway, dining table to the left, sitting room at the far end with floor to ceiling industrial style windows. The rest was warm wood panelling, mid-century wood and olive green velvet furniture and a set of three massive paintings of cloud streaked skies.

'It looks like it's straight out of a magazine. Maybe he is gay,' Jaq said, glancing back into the bedroom and running her eye over the perfectly made bed.

Darren gave a cynical laugh and said, 'My Brenda would kill to have a place decorated like this, although hers would be fuller of knick knacks. I wish she'd be more minimalist.'

Jaq laughed. She was all too familiar with Darren's wife's passion for interior decorating.

Now she headed for the kitchen to look through the cupboards. It could be very revealing to see what a suspect had in the cupboards. Kitchens were often used as hiding spaces for all sorts of things, from drugs to keys and weapons. Often mixed in with something innocuous, like the flour or the sugar.

Simon White's kitchen was as minimalist as the rest of the flat. He had a small stack of plates, minimal cutlery, and barely any food. Milk and bread in the fridge and a box of tea in the cupboard above the kettle, along with four packets of dried fruit, one apple, one pear, one mango and a half-empty bag of crystallised ginger. All too small to hide anything else in it. There was no flour, sugar, bags of pasta, cans of sauce or any of the detritus of most people's kitchens.

'This makes it look like he doesn't live here at all,' Jaq said, and might have added more, but her phone went off.

'Yes, Amber?'

'Boss, I think I may have found something weird.'

'Ok, just a sec.'

Jaq pushed Darren into the bedroom, closed the door behind them and switched the phone to speaker.

'This Simon White, you asked me to look into... It all looked pretty normal, no criminal convictions, not even the proverbial parking ticket. But it looks like your man may have changed his name as part of the witness protection programme.'

'Really? When?' Jaq asked, looking at Darren with the sort of, what do we have here expression.

'Hard to tell, but there are no records of him from around fifteen years ago. Nothing obvious, although Simon White is a pretty common name.'

'Okay, thanks, keep digging and let me know if you turn anything else up.'

'Will do,' Amber said, and the phone clicked off.

'Well, what do you think of that?' Jaq said and cocked her head at Darren.

'Tenuous, people land up in witness protection for many reasons and I'm guessing he's in his thirties, so if he changed his name so long ago, it was probably because of something that happened when he was a kid.'

'What though?' Jaq said as she took in the minimalist bedroom, with another pair of sky paintings and the same floor to ceiling windows. 'If it was a sexual offence, it might be relevant.'

'It isn't much to go on,' Darren said. 'Liz Chadwick was last seen near his house. He might have a record and he's a colleague of the missing woman.'

'He's super nervous and his flat is unnaturally clean.'

'Some people are just neat freaks.'

'I think we should take him in, just in case.' Police were unfair and harsh, but there was a reason for it, mostly because they were trying to protect the weak and the vulnerable or to get justice. Sometimes that prevented them from showing compassion for potential suspects. 'We need to keep him where we can see him and where he can't do any damage limitations or just vanish on us.'

'It will have to be voluntary. If you can convince him to come to the station, I'll go along with it.'

'Alright,' Jaq said and went back to Simon. 'Mr White, we'd like you to come down to the station to answer some questions. We'd also appreciate if you let us take your security recordings and all your unwashed clothes for forensic analysis.'

It was a long shot. Without a warrant, Simon White was within his rights to tell her to go to hell and chuck the lot of them out.

He looked up, pale and shaky.

'I didn't do anything. You're wasting your time and Liz's looking into me.'

'All the same, sir.'

Simon White stared at her, it seemed in a blank, thoughts flickering across his face. She held her breath, waiting for him to tell her to go to hell.

But in the end he seemed to crumple, shrugged and said, 'Do whatever you want.'

'Thank you. This way, sir.'

Keeping it polite never hurt. Sometimes it really annoyed Jaq to have to do it when she had just arrested someone she knew damn well to be guilty, but that wasn't the case here. So she was keeping her expressions neutral. She didn't want to give Simon White any sign of whether she thought him innocent or guilty.

3

D ESPITE THE DISTANCE OF only three blocks between his house and the station, they drove back.

'If you wouldn't mind,' Jaq said as she ushered White into the station and past the argumentative drunks, who were yelling at the desk sergeant, 'We'd like it if a police surgeon looked over your body.'

'What?' White said, staring at.

'It's all for your own benefit and protection, sir,' Jaq said, giving him a slight, nothing to worry about here, smile. 'If there are no scratches or marks on your body, it will be a point in your favour.'

White looked like he didn't understand.

'It will only take a moment,' Jaq said and to her surprise, he gave a nod.

So she walked him down to the police surgeon's cubicle.

'He's very docile, isn't he?' Darren said when Jaq rejoined him at their desks.

Jaq nodded, noting that they were the only team that was back, and Amber was by whatever was on her computer. 'But also scared shitless. You see how he's shaking, and that look in his eyes, like he's not altogether here.'

'Too scared. I've seen plenty of innocent people afraid they were about to be fitted up. I've seen guilty people in tears because they've been caught. But this guy is genuinely terrified, only I can't work out the reason, innocent or guilty.'

'Same,' Jaq said, and put her updates into the team database on the case before checking all the new information from the other teams. There wasn't much yet, so she was glad to see the surgeon stroll in.

'Anything? Any scratches or bruises to indicate he's been involved in a fight?'

'Not so much as a razor burn,' the surgeon said. 'Although your man's been through the wars. Looks like he tried to slit his wrists at least once in the past, maybe twice. He was also a victim of violence, most likely domestic. He's got cigarette burns all over his body.'

'Not self harm?' Darren asked.

'Not the ones on his back, at any rate, and nothing recent.'

'Fine, then let's stick him into the interview room and let him stew for now.'

'Okay,' Jaq said and followed the doctor back to his cubicle, where Simon White emerged from behind the screen, his clothes all neatly arranged. He was definitely a tidy one. 'Now, if you wouldn't mind, Mr White, we'd appreciate it if you could answer a few of our questions.'

'Oh... okay,' Simon said, giving her a hopeless look.

At least he was still being cooperative.

Jaq showed Simon into a grey, featureless, soundproofed interrogation room and said, 'I'll just get someone to rustle you up a cup of tea. It's been a long night after all. I won't be a sec,' and she closed the door on him before he could object.

Then Jaq hurried to the room next door, where Darren was already watching White through the one-way mirror. It was useful to understand the mental state of the person they were going to interview and, with Simon, get a handle on why he was so nervous.

Some people were cocky bastards who would take a stroll about the room and check themselves out in the mirror. Most stayed put in the chair, but looked about. Simon sat slumped in the chair. His chin rested on his chest so that they couldn't see his face. He gripped his hands in his lap, and his right leg jumped incessantly.

'Yeah, scared shitless,' Darren said.

A uniformed officer entered the interview room and deposited a paper cup of black tea, with a sachet of milk and another of sugar beside it and withdrew. Simon didn't even glance at the tea, never mind make a move to drink it.

'Alright, let's do a bit more digging,' Jaq said and headed back into the open plan office.

While it was a cruel tactic to leave someone to stew, it was effective. It gave people time to consider what they should do next, what to divulge and what to keep secret and what to say to wriggle out of the situation. Then, by the time a cop sat down opposite them, they'd blurt everything out. They might believe they were being clever, but they usually landed up saying more than they should.

'I've found something,' Amber said. She pulled a chair over from the opposite desk and sat with Jaq to her left and Darren to her right. 'Your man changed his name when he was still a teenager. It turns out he's actually Adrian Black, and he has quite the record.'

Amber was beaming at them as if she'd just uncovered a gold mine.

'Adrian Black? Is that supposed to mean something to me?' Jaq asked.

'Maybe not, but I'm sure you've heard of Doctor Gregory Black.'

It didn't even need a second to work through her mental files for that one.

'The serial killer!?' Jaq said and looked up into Darren's equally astonished face.

'He's the son.'

'Didn't Gregory Black use his son to lure in the women he murdered?' Darren asked.

'Yeah,' Jaq said. 'He staged him like a traffic accident victim. They kidnapped the women who hurried over to help. They were then assaulted and finally murdered. I can't believe the son of Gregory Black, the most prolific serial killer the Midlands has ever seen, is sitting in our interrogation room.'

'It explains why he looks so nervous, though,' Darren said. 'I wouldn't want anyone to know I had that kind of past, either.'

'And he got a record from that?'

'They prosecuted him under the joint enterprise law,' Amber said, looking over her notes. 'But because he was only fourteen, appeared as a witness against his father, and was also a victim of abuse, they only gave him three years in a juvenile detention centre.'

'And after that, nothing?' Daren asked.

'Squeaky clean, boss.'

'Or just very careful,' Jaq said, 'after all, his father was able to keep killing for four years. Who knows what his son learned from that?'

'I know you like playing the devil's advocate, Burnham, but that may be taking it too far.'

'What we need is somebody to tell us what kind of person Simon White is.'

'While you figure that out, I'll check the list of local sex offenders, and see who we look at next.'

Jaq nodded and considered a bit. It was late, two am, but there was somebody who might be able to help. She called up the database with the phone numbers of all the prison directors and called her.

'Do you know what time it is?' an annoyed voice said on the phone. 'This better be an emergency.'

'I'm sorry to bother you, Director Strange, but we have a missing woman. Currently, I've got Simon White, AKA Adrian Black, in custody.'

'Simon?' Director Strange said, and she actually sounded surprised.

'I don't need details of his crime. I just want to know whether, in your opinion, Simon or Adrian might commit a similar crime to that of his father's?'

'You mean in line with the abused becoming an abuser?' The director asked, and she sounded even more tired. 'I'd say that's unlikely. The young men who come to my facility fall into two categories. Those who will become lifelong criminals and those whose experiences inoculate them against that life and who will go straight. Especially as he was more a victim than anything else. Adrian's behaviour after leaving the centre bears that out, don't you agree?'

'Yeah, it does look like it.'

'Detective Inspector Burnham, we don't just incarcerate troubled youth at young offenders' institutes, we also provide counselling, education and emotional support. All of which Simon desperately needed because his life before he came to us was brutal, absolutely brutal. My staff and I spent three years putting that boy back together again. It was slow, and it was difficult. Even when he was with us, he overdosed twice. I hope, therefore, that whatever you're doing won't crush him.'

'I understand, thank you, Director Strange,' Jaq said, and hung up to find Darren watching her with a questioning expression on his face. 'He's been stewing for two hours. Should we go speak to him?'

'Why not?' Darren said.

Simon White was sitting in exactly the same position as when they'd led him into the room. The tea was untouched.

'That will be stone cold by now,' Jaq said, and flagged down a uniform to bring in another.

'Have you found Liz?' Simon asked, looking up.

There was a tremor in his voice.

'I'm afraid not.' Jaq took the left seat opposite White, with Darren on her right. 'I'd like to thank you for your cooperation, Simon. You don't mind if I call you Simon, do you?'

Simon shook his head.

'I know this must be very stressful for you, but you understand that we have to do everything we can to find Liz.'

'Yes,' Simon whispered and his gaze dropped back to his hands clasped in his lap.

So Jaq started the questioning, about Simon's relationship with Liz, how they got on at work, why she might have been near his house, even his daily routine. He answered everything without hesitation, although his right leg kept drumming away.

Finally, Jaq and Darren had no more questions.

'Can I get you something to eat? You must be hungry, a sandwich or something?'

Simon looked up, making eye contact for the first time.

'You're wasting time. I have nothing to do with Liz's disappearance and I've done everything I can to help. I've answered all your questions and let you take whatever you wanted from my house. But if you fixate on me, it will be no help finding Liz. Please, don't do this.'

'Don't worry,' Jaq said. 'Talking to you is only one strand of our investigation. We are doing everything possible to find Liz, I promise you.'

'We've made it a big strand,' Darren said once they were clear of the interview room. 'So far we have nothing else, and neither do the other teams.'

'But I'm not feeling it with him either. Do you think we should send his clothes for DNA analysis?'

'Not yet,' Daren said. 'Our budget for forensic services is tight. We'll only send the clothes through if we can find something else to tie this particular suspect to Elizabeth Chadwick's disappearance.'

'Then I guess the next thing is his surveillance footage,' Jaq said. 'Why do you think he's got cameras filming himself? That's weird, isn't it?'

'Helpful for him in this kind of situation. It shows him coming home, checking his video feed and going to bed, every day without fail, and it shows that he never left his house on Saturday.'

'Really? The whole day, what was he doing?'

'Looks like he was painting,' Darren said. 'The only place his surveillance breaks down is at the point where his light goes off. If he had some way to switch it off the recording from his bed, he could easily get up in the dark and leave his house with nobody knowing.'

'So not that useful. Just strange.'

'I've got a couple of uniforms going right back through past recordings, just in case. Stranger than the cameras is that he doesn't seem to have any visitors. The only people who come to his door are delivery men and even that isn't very frequent, just the odd takeaway, or parcel delivery.'

'Okay people, attention,' Detective Chief Inspector Morris said, banging on the side of the board until everyone was looking his way. 'I have great news. We've found Elizabeth Chadwick.'

Jaq let out a relieved sigh and rolled her head back, staring at the ceiling.

'Thank God.'

'Yeah,' Darren said, grinning from ear to ear and barely paying any attention to what Morris was adding about where and how she'd been found. 'If uniforms had done their jobs properly, we wouldn't have landed up working through the night. Anyway, you'd best release our suspect. Or rather, ex suspect.'

'With profuse apologies,' Jaq said.

It wasn't the first time she was having to say sorry to somebody they'd hauled in, and she never feel guilty about doing it. It was police procedure to bring in anyone remotely suspicious, and Simon fitted the bill. She also wondered about him and his background. Could he really be a law-abiding citizen with a past like his? It seemed unlikely and something that needed further investigation.

Simon hadn't been this terrified in years. He'd never reached a state of peace. That was probably asking too much. But he'd been told things would get better and gradually they had.

Now this. He felt like someone had thrown him back in time. Back to when he was helpless and terrified and alone. His hands were shaking so hard he couldn't get them to be still, no matter how tightly he clenched them against his body. His leg was the same. The interview room was almost identical to the one they had held him in when his father–

He cut that thought off. It was too much to go there. His shrink had told him that reliving something in your memory just burned it deeper into your brain and that he didn't want.

Dr Nobel had told him to take long deep breaths to release... something, some calming hormone. But deep breaths wouldn't cut it. He needed something stronger, some anti-anxiety drug.

And Liz... what had happened to Liz? Was she dead? He knew little about her, aside from what he'd learned at work, but people wouldn't care about that.

It was nearly Monday too, wasn't it? They had hauled him off in his slobbing about the house sweats and a long-sleeved t-shirt and his other clothes were sitting in a bag somewhere waiting for DNA analysis. Thank god he hadn't been put into one of those lime green paper forensic suits as they had done to him when he was a kid.

What would everyone at work think, though? Did they know Liz was missing? They had to, right?

The police were probably questioning all of them, too. But what about when Monday rolled around? Would he be free to go to work? If he didn't, they'd notice he was missing, too. Then they'd talk, wondering where he was, and why he wasn't there.

Would the cops tell the company he was "helping with their enquiries"? God, he hoped not. What would he do then?

If Liz was dead and he went back to the office, what would they think? No smoke without fire? He was always a bit odd, kept himself to himself, wasn't really sociable?

Christ, he'd been so careful. He'd tried so hard to keep himself safe and now somebody had gone missing and who had they homed in on? How could this be happening?

'Mr White?'

The voice came from far away. He turned and everything was hazy. He had to blink for his vision to clear and he realised it was D.I. Burnham, leaning down to look at his face, a slight smile of concern on hers.

'You've had a rough time, huh?'

'What?'

Simon's voice was tight and croaky. His tongue was dry and felt stiff.

'You're the kind who shuts down under stress, aren't you?'

Burnham waved her hand at the cold cup of tea, and a white bread sandwich whose edges had dried and curled. He couldn't even remember when that had appeared.

'I'm a stress eater myself,' the detective carried on.

Simon didn't get it. She was talking to him like the social worker who'd sat in with him when he was questioned as a kid. Was she trying this other tack because the last one had failed?

'Here, your clothes.' Burnham handed him a clear plastic bag containing his laundry. 'We'll return your computer at the door.'

'You're letting me go?' Simon asked, because he really wasn't sure what was going on.

'You were never under arrest, Mr White. You could have left at any time.'

The police were funny that way, giving one impression when they meant the opposite. So devious. He pushed himself to his feet, surprised at how hard that was to do. How many hours had he been sitting there? His legs were cramping and unwilling to stretch out.

'Liz?'

It was probably stupid to ask, but he had to know. Mainly because he was scared shitless for her. But also because he needed to know what to expect when he went back to work. If he went back to work.

'We've found her.'

The detective spoke in a neutral voice that didn't bode well.

'Is she... is she dead?' Simon asked, the last word coming out as a whisper.

'She's alive, but injured. It turns out she caught a cab somewhere near your house in a CCTV black spot, so we didn't see that. The cab got into an accident and Liz's bag got lost so the hospital couldn't identify her. Thankfully, we've now done so.'

'She's alive.' Simon collapsed back onto the chair, sank his head into his arms and sobbed, wave after wave of relief rolling over him. 'Thank God!'

'Listen, I know it's only three blocks away, but let me drive you home,' Burnham said.

Simon didn't want the policewoman to take him home. He wanted nothing more to do with her. But he also felt like he couldn't get home on his own, no matter how short the walk. He was feeling lightheaded and so weak he had serious doubts about making it all the way upstairs.

'Here, drink this.' Burnham twisted the cap off a bottle of coke and handed it to him. 'You've been under a lot of stress and haven't touched a thing in hours. You're probably feeling nauseous because of it.'

Simon didn't want the drink, but had to admit that he felt better after downing it and was strong enough to get back onto his feet.

'Come on, this way,' Burnham said and walked off without looking back.

She said nothing as she opened her car door for him. Thankfully, not a police car with all the accompanying livery. And she said nothing on the short drive home.

Once she pulled into the parking lot, Simon gave her a nod of thanks as he got out, clutching his bag of belongings.

'I'll make sure you get in safely,' Burnham said with that same, mildly concerned smile she'd given him at the station.

He didn't have the energy to tell her not to bother, and by the time he got to the top floor, he was too exhausted to say anything. He was used to the daily climb, but he had to hand it to the detective; she reached the top without looking winded. She then insisted on accompanying him to his door. It was midmorning; the sun was already up, and a couple of neighbours passed him and gave him a curious once over. They'd be gossiping about him for a while, too. He hoped he wouldn't have to move.

'Thanks, I can take it from here,' Simon said as he opened his door and stepped inside.

'I'm sure you can, but you've been up overnight, so I just want to make sure you're comfortable before I leave.'

I'd be a damn sight more comfortable without you, Simon thought but was too tired to say so. He just left the door open for the detective to follow him in.

'Would you like something to eat?' Burnham said. 'Or I can fix you a cup of tea?'

Now Simon was confused. Was this how the police usually treated suspects? Or was this only the treatment you got if they wrongfully accused you? Maybe she didn't want to get sued for police brutality.

'I don't want anything,' he muttered.

Least of all from her.

'I thought you'd like to know that we informed your employer that you were helping with our enquiries. And that obviously, now that Liz has been found, you're in the clear. We stressed this was all routine procedure and that it was just bad luck that Liz disappeared near your house.'

'Okay,' Simon said, too tired and eager for the detective to leave to care about what she was saying.

'Are you sure you don't want anything to eat or drink?'

'I'm sure.'

'Okay, well, get some sleep. It's what I'm going to do now too,' the detective said with a final, sympathetic smile, and then she was gone, pulling the door shut behind her.

Simon made sure the door was locked, ripped off his clothes that now reeked of sweat, crawled under his duvet. Considering how tired he was, it took a long time before he fell asleep.

4

—·—

T HE MOMENT A PALE grey dawn light filtered into his
room, Simon gave up on trying to sleep. It had been
fitful and filled with nightmares. He glanced at the clock:
4:30 am. There was no point in staying in bed, so he took
a long shower.

At 5:30, he was clean, dressed, sitting at his dining table,
barely noticing the cup of tea warming his hands. He'd
added more lumps of ginger than usual because he was
feeling nauseous. Dr Noble had told him, years ago, that
ginger helped calm the stomach. It usually worked for him.
Today it was having no effect.

Simon gazed into the depths of the mug and thought
about the coming day. He'd be going back to work and
everyone was bound to know that he'd spent the previous
night in police custody. Both thoughts, what lay ahead and
what had just happened, made his hand shake, so he put
the mug down.

Simon glanced at the big clock hanging on the kitchen
wall. He placed it so that you could see it from any part of
the open plan living area. It was 5:38.

He couldn't go to work. He was too exhausted to
concentrate on anything. That was an excuse. He was
scared shitless about what people would think. Would

they be wondering why he'd been called in and not anybody else? Would they be casting glances his way and whispering?

He'd worked so hard not to stand out. To be an anonymous office worker that nobody gave a second thought to. Now this? Everyone would know, wouldn't they? Then, anytime something odd happened, they'd go back to wondering about him.

The anxiety he thought he'd overcome was bobbing just below the surface, and he couldn't control it. He didn't want to admit it, but he needed help and he had only one place to get it.

At 9am on the dot, Simon phoned Dr Nobel's office for an appointment. Thankfully, the receptionist said he could see her right away. Then he phoned the office and took the rest of the week off. Since he'd already planned and booked all his holidays, he wondered whether they'd be okay with it.

'Are you alright, Simon?' Sarah asked, much to his surprise.

'Fine,' he muttered, 'just exhausted.'

'Take whatever time you need.'

Simon stared in surprise at his mobile once he'd hung up. He'd expected more suspicion and push back. Was it a good sign or a bad that Sarah had given him the leave without question?

'Come in, Simon,' Dr Nobel said as she held the door open with a welcoming smile.

'Thanks.' Simon failed to hold the eye contact, his gaze sweeping the familiar walls of books, the window surrounded by potted plants and one of his earliest sunset sky paintings hanging behind the desk. 'Sorry for showing up so suddenly.'

'You know you're always welcome here,' Dr Nobel said.

Simon wished he didn't need that kind of reassurance, but today he did. He glanced up at Dr Nobel as he sat down on her leather sofa and was struck, as he was every time he saw her, by how kind she looked. She had snow white hair cut into a bob that usually brushed her shoulders. Today she'd tied it back in a ponytail. Her face was round and fair with rosy cheeks, and she had blue eyes that could look vague or drill right through you.

Simon shuddered as the memory of his first meeting with Dr Nobel hit him with the force of a high-speed train. The police had smashed down the door to his father's house in the middle of the night. Not being found out was something Gregory Black obsessed about. All his instructions revolved around what Simon could or couldn't do to ensure their safety.

So he acted on instinct as the cries of 'Police, nobody move,' followed the splintering of the door.

Simon rolled out of bed, slipped underneath and curled into a terrified ball against the wall at the headboard end. He'd held his breath as his bedroom door swung open and the light flicked on.

'Holy crap,' somebody muttered. 'Kid's room, we've got a kid's room,' the man shouted.

'Does he have a kid?' somebody else asked.

'It would have to be a fucking disturbed one,' the first voice said and Simon watched a pair of laced up black boots approach his bed. 'Still warm.'

Then a torch flashed under the bed, dazzling Simon so he couldn't see who was holding it.

'Shit, there's a kid down here!'

Simon had expected to be hauled out from under the bed, the way his father did when he was enraged. But the torch and feet disappeared and nothing happened for what felt like an eternity.

Then Dr Nobel had arrived, looking the same as she did now and sat down on the floor, her back against the side of his bed.

'I'm Dr Helen Nobel,' she'd said. 'What's your name?'

Simon had been so terrified he couldn't speak, torn between his dread of what his father might say to him later and what the police would do to him now.

'You're quite the artist, aren't you?' Dr Nobel had said, waving her arm to encompass the walls of Simon's room.

He'd covered them in drawings from the floor up to the height of his reach. Later, he'd learned that forensic scientists had photographed every inch of the walls and they had used his images in Gregory Black's trial. Simon hadn't drawn for that reason, but he'd pretty much recorded everything he'd seen and done with his father.

He was processing his thoughts, Dr Nobel had told him years later. It was something people did when they didn't have the words from lack of experience or ability to talk about what they had been through. She'd encouraged him to carry on drawing and, especially in the early years, they had communicated that way, Simon explaining what his various sketches meant.

'So what happened?' Dr Nobel asked, bringing Simon back to the present.

He took a deep breath, drawing together his scattered thoughts. 'I hit a brick wall.'

'Come again?'

'Remember when I told you I no longer needed therapy? You said that I shouldn't throw away your number?'

'You said you were doing fine and didn't need my help anymore.'

'Was I too cocky?'

'Not at all. I'm always pleased when my patients feel confident enough to face the world without me.'

'But you said at the time that one day I might hit a brick wall and then I should call you.'

'I'm glad you remembered. So what is this particular brick wall?'

Simon clasped his hands in his lap because they'd started to shake and stopped his right leg from bouncing. It was hard to come to the point.

'I got arrested.' Dr Nobel looked so astonished that Simon hurriedly added. 'No, I was, "helping the police with their enquiries".'

'Good Lord, why?'

'A colleague went missing. They've found her now. She had an accident. Nothing to do with me. But till they found her... I don't know if they figured out who I was... they didn't say anything about that and I didn't either. But... sitting in the interrogation room.' Simon couldn't go on and dropped his gaze to the red and blue Persian rug.

'I imagine that brought back a lot of unpleasant memories,' Dr Nobel said.

It was the king of understatements.

'It isn't only that. What will my colleagues think of the fact that they hauled me into the station?'

'Will the colleague who vanished be back at work too?'

'I don't know... she was hospitalised.'

'Ah, then it may take a while. I'm sure they will be more sympathetic over what you went through than anything else. Either way, you don't need to worry about them. As far as they are concerned, you are merely a designer with as simple a life history as their own. Have they ever asked you about your life?'

'Less than I expected. I stuck with the story we came up with that I was orphaned at fourteen and grew up in a home after that.'

'It is mostly true,' Dr Nobel said. 'Fabrications are best if they contain an element of truth. There was no point in pretending you had a normal childhood.'

Simon nodded. The orphan part was true: his father had committed suicide within months of being sentenced to life imprisonment. Dr Nobel had come straight to see him at the young offender's institute to tell him about it and provide support.

He'd been more affected by the monster's death than he'd expected. He'd been filled with a strange mixture of relief and pain that he still couldn't understand.

'You look exhausted,' Dr Nobel said, her voice softening.

'I couldn't sleep after...'

'I'll give you a prescription for the anxiety. It will help you sleep. Don't take too many and only when you feel they're necessary.'

Simon nodded. It was what the doctor always told him, and he tried to abide by her guidelines.

'And you should eat more. I'm worried about how thin you've got.'

'I'll try.'

'Don't try. Do,' Dr Nobel said back to her firm doctor's voice. 'Now tell me about the rest of your life. Are you still creating your wonderful sky paintings?'

5

— . —

'WHAT DO YOU THINK?' Sarah asked as she did a slow graceful walk around the fitting room, showing off her lacy, ivory wedding dress that glowed in the sun coming through the tall sash windows.

'Beautiful,' Jaq said, suppressing a twinge of jealousy.

Was she ever going to be a bride, or was she doomed to always be the bridesmaid? Not that she intended to have a traditional wedding. Now wasn't the time to feel sorry for herself, anyway. She was here to support Sarah.

The seamstress, who'd been watching from a distance, gave a happy nod and said, 'It's all fitting perfectly now. So whatever you do, don't lose any more weight, or your dress will look baggy.'

Sarah gave a guilty nod, and Jaq grinned at her. Sarah had been dieting so religiously that they'd not even met up for a coffee after the engagement party.

'Okay, no more dieting,' Sarah promised the seamstress as she followed her out to the changing room.

Jaq doubted it and even though Sarah was probably within the normal weight range, she knew her best friend well enough to know she'd continue starving herself until the wedding. Now she leaned back as much as she could on the elegant velvet chair reserved for friends and family to attend the fittings, and her eyes ran along the rungs and rungs of dresses in all possible shades of white. Most seemed to be ballgown style, and very frothy. A few were the more figure hugging sheath like dresses that Jaq favoured.

She couldn't sit still so strolled over to get a closer look and pretend she was buying a dress. It was a ridiculous waste of money. Why pay thousands of pounds for a dress you were only ever going to wear once?

Her sister's dress, a beautiful creation, now occupied an inordinate amount of space at the end of her wardrobe where its plastic cover had still not protected it from the grubby fingers of her four-year-old nephew. He was soon to be joined by a sister, so even less chance of wearing a beautiful wedding dress then.

Maybe that was also why Jaq was feeling like she was running out of time. Not only her older sister, but even some of her friends had started to have kids. She was way behind them, and feeling more left out by the day.

Maybe this was why she'd agreed to meet up with Rob, Sarah and Aaron this evening for a couple's dinner. It felt far too early for something like that, especially since she hadn't had a chance to ask why Sarah had rolled her eyes about Rob.

Since it was fresh in her mind, she said the moment Sarah emerged from the changing rooms, back in her casual weekend attire, 'I've got a bone to pick with you.'

'You have?' Sarah asked, her expression turning to one of mild confusion as she tried to work out what she'd done wrong.

'You gave me a signal about Rob at your drinks do, and now you've set up this couple's date, so I don't know what to think.'

'Oh,' Sarah said, and she blushed rosily as she linked her arm in Jaq's and led her out of the shop and down the narrow stairs, onto the Kensington street. 'Let's get a coffee and I'll explain. It's too early to be meeting the guys, anyway.'

'And you'll be drinking it black,' Jaq said with a laugh.

'I know, I know. I was told not to lose any more weight, but honestly, I'm terrified of gaining what I've lost between now and the wedding and not being able to get into the dress at all.'

'You'll be fine,' Jaq said and made her way to a decent-looking coffee shop that had the virtues of not being a chain and having table service. 'Now spill.'

Sarah settled at right angles to Jaq and gave a slight shrug.

'Rob is Aaron's friend. That's why you were invited. Aaron is playing matchmaker.'

'Because?'

'Because Rob is also desperate for a partner. He's been alternating between teasing Aaron about getting married and begging Aaron to set him up with one of my friends.'

'So why don't you like Rob?'

'Rob's a little... how do I explain? He's always the best, I guess. Since he's a man, they're better than women, since he's living in London it's the greatest city in the world, since he plays rugby it's the best sport and anyone who does anything else for exercise is wasting their time.'

'In other words, he's full of himself.'

Sarah shrugged in grudging agreement, then ordered her black coffee while Jaq got a latte.

'He's a very good salesman, and they have to project an air of confidence and make you feel good about buying whatever he's selling. It can make them all rather arrogant.'

'Even Aaron?' Jaq said, because she couldn't resist teasing her.

'Just a bit. But Aaron is always at the top of the sales league, so he's less boastful.'

'Ah well. I guess I'll see what I think after today's dinner,' Jaq said, and went back to contemplating the foam on her coffee. 'Can I ask you a question about Simon White?'

'Simon? I thought you weren't interested in him. It would be a waste of time, even if you were.'

'All the same, I'm curious,' Jaq said, glancing at the surrounding tables. It was a quiet afternoon with only a handful of people, mostly women. 'What is he like as an employee? You're his boss, aren't you?'

'He's excellent,' Sarah said without hesitation. 'The best designer we've got, and it's not just because he can draw well. He understands our client's briefs and does things with the brief that just leave the rest of us in awe. My work always looks okay until I compare it to Simon's, then I feel so pedestrian.'

'I always thought you were hugely talented. And at least you have people skills.'

'Oh... Simon has those, too. He isn't shy. I like taking him along to client meetings because he's perfectly comfortable dealing with people on all levels and he won't let people push him around.'

'How do you mean?'

'I guess... it's the opposite of Rob, who's always bragging about his achievements. Simon will listen and smile politely when people brag, but he doesn't engage in the willy waving that sometimes goes on with men. He defers to me in meetings, but also makes it clear he expects the other men in the room to do the same. It's hard to describe exactly, but he's got an inner strength that most men don't have. It's a kind of take it or leave it attitude.'

'Really? He didn't seem that way when we took him in,' Jaq said, genuinely surprised.

Then again, Simon had been quite clear about not wanting her to help him out at home.

'I'm not surprised with you. You hauled him in for questioning. Who on earth could take that in their stride?'

'So there's nothing that puts you on edge about him?'

'Jaq... what is this really about? You're starting to sound like you're interrogating me.'

'Oh, it's nothing, never mind.'

It worried Jaq that her best friend was working with somebody with such a troubled past, but confidentiality meant she couldn't say anything. If Simon really was reformed and not a threat to anyone, it was unfair to him, too.

'Is there something I should know about Simon?' Sarah asked, looking genuinely concerned.

'No, don't worry. I just wondered since he was so nervous at the interview.'

'He took the week off too,' Sarah said. 'Even though he books his holidays at the beginning of the year and had everything allocated. So I knew something was wrong. You weren't really horrible to him, were you?'

'Of course not.'

Sarah rarely asked Jaq about her work, probably because she knew how difficult it could be, and she was too kindhearted to hear about how suspects were treated. Detective shows sometimes had the protagonist try to set people's minds at ease.

In reality, she couldn't even do that for victims, lest they were involved. She had to remain objective and withhold her empathy. She couldn't offer false hope or even give off sympathetic body language. It was harsh, but it was necessary.

———

'Simon!' Sarah said the moment he walked into the office.

So no chance now of slipping silently to his desk, especially as everyone else had looked up too. He felt his hand tremble, so tightened his grip on his satchel's strap to hide it as he glanced from Sara to the rest of the team and back to Sarah. He hadn't known what to expect, but suspicion was what he anticipated. Only now, they all looked glad.

'It's good to see you back,' Sarah said, following along behind him.

Pam and Hilda joined her, both saying, 'Simon, Simon, we missed you.'

'They needed your design genius,' John said.

At least he hadn't joined the group that was following Simon to his desk. It was second to last along a row of double desks in their open plan office. Sarah, as team leader, had the end desk nearest the window that looked out onto a boring office dominated street, but if she leaned her chair far back enough, she could peek through a gap between two buildings and see St Pauls.

'Let me get you a cup of tea. You'll need it after all that stress,' Hilda said.

'That was last week,' Simon said, glancing at Liz's desk, that was conspicuously empty.

'All the same, the police are brutes. I hope they didn't threaten you?'

'No, they were really polite.'

It was the truth, even if it had felt threatening at the time. Simon guessed his father's conditioning that had drilled into him the police were to be avoided at all costs, had embedded itself into his psyche.

'It was just police procedure. Simon was merely unlucky he lived so close to where Liz went missing,' Sarah said, returning to her desk and smiling up at him over the low dividers they had that supposedly provided some privacy but didn't prevent conversation. 'Now let's get back to work and leave Simon to unpack.'

'With tea,' Hilda said, depositing a mug of milky white tea on his desk.

Simon preferred stronger tea with only a dash of milk. While the rest of his teammates knew that, Hilda just kept making tea the way she liked it.

Simon glanced at Liz's desk again and wondered when she'd come back. He didn't think he'd be able to believe she was okay until he saw her with his own eyes. But he felt too awkward to ask about her.

Just then the creak of crutches drew everyone's attention back to their sliding glass doors and Liz stepped inside, her leg in a cast, and a large plaster covering her left cheek, but otherwise looking fine and grinning from ear to ear.

'Liz!' everyone shouted.

'Oh, yeah, hi,' Liz said with an embarrassed wave. 'I'm sorry I caused you so much trouble,' she said, turning to Simon.

'Oh, uh, it couldn't be helped,' Simon said, aware every eye in the room was now on him. 'I'm really glad you're okay. At least... you are okay, aren't you?'

'Just a bit dinged up, but it doesn't hurt anymore, so they gave me permission to come back. I dread to think how much work has piled up in my absence.'

'It's fine,' Sarah said. 'We could have coped without you for a while longer. If you find yourself flagging, feel free to go home early.'

'But go home,' Hilda said. 'What were you even doing near Simon's? Is there a little hush-hush thing going on between the two of you?'

Simon blinked at Hilda in amazement, shaking his head. Liz looked like she was squirming with embarrassment.

'I was actually on my way to see my boyfriend. I didn't know Simon's flat was so close by.'

'It's fine, no need to explain,' Simon said and turned on his massive computer monitor as a hope that people would take the hint and go back to work.

'Maybe just ask your boyfriend to move,' Pam said, and everybody laughed.

Simon was just glad to get confirmation Liz was okay. He'd been having difficulty sleeping, and was off his food too, despite Dr Nobel's orders. He hoped Liz being back would put an end to his own anxiety induced restlessness.

For now, he popped half a dozen lumps of crystallised ginger into his tea, gave it a stir and started on the mountain of emails that had stacked up during his absence.

6

JAQ REWOUND THE INTERVIEW tapes and rubbed her eyes tiredly before watching it over again, looking for any slip-ups during the interrogation. The case was one of the worst, a missing boy. Two older boys from the same school had spirited him away. Brad Davis was twelve years old and had last been captured on CCTV, being intimidated by the two suspects outside a corner shop, and then being led away by them. Brad had looked terrified.

So far, the investigating team had the CCTV footage and the missing boy's blood on the suspect's clothes. But the two steadfastly denied everything, even that they knew Brad. Since Jaq and Darren had been allocated the interrogation, it was up to them to get the boys to talk.

The rest of the team searched the area where Brad had last been seen, questioned friends and relatives, analysed reams of social media posts and did anything and everything that could help them find Brad. Hopefully, still alive, although the blood spatter was worrying.

'Nothing we say gets through to either of those two,' Jaq said as she glared at the computer monitors displaying the two boys, each seated in an interrogation room, accompanied by a social worker and a family member.

The big burly kid, Chazza, slumped on the desk, his head buried in his arms. The smaller, rat-like Miles was wide awake despite the hours they'd spent questioning him and looking about as if plotting his escape.

Darren stared at his chunky watch, his lips moving as he calculated how much longer they could hold the kids.

'Well?' Jaq asked.

'Five hours and twenty-seven minutes.'

'Damn, and the social workers won't allow them to spend a second more than that, either.'

Darren ran a hand over his stubbled head and said, 'I'm stumped. They won't shift, the social workers just obstruct us and the psychological profiler hasn't given us anything that's helped. At this rate, we'll never find that kid.'

'Do you think he's still alive?'

'God, I hope so,' Darren said.

As the father of three teenage sons, this case was hitting particularly close to home for him.

'There is still one possibility, but it's one hell of a long shot.'

Jaq had been sitting on the idea for a while, and until now, she'd decided against mentioning it every time it surfaced. Now they had nothing else.

'Let's hear it,' Darren said, rubbing his tired eyes.

'Simon White.'

'The serial killer's son? I don't see what use he would be?'

'He spent time at a young offenders' institute.'

'So you think he might scare them into saying something to reduce their sentences? That really is a long shot, especially as we have nothing concrete to nail the little shits with.'

'He lives close enough that it won't be a bother to get him to come here, will it?'

'It's one in the morning.'

'If we explain the urgency of the situation, I'm sure he'll understand.'

'I'm not so sure he will,' Darren said, but shrugged. 'What the hell, aside from having a last go at the kids ourselves, and praying the team going over the CCTV footage finds something, we've got nothing better right now.'

Jaq pulled on a jumper as she followed Darren out. She really was clutching at straws, but she would do whatever it took to try to find Brad. If she discovered more out about Simon into the bargain, all the better because the more she thought about it, the stranger his life and behaviour seemed.

They drove to Simon White's place again. It wouldn't save them many minutes, but it would save some.

'God damn, that's a lot of stairs,' Darren muttered as he headed for the wide concrete stairs that formed a square tower up to the fourth floor. 'I forgot about those when I agreed to come over.'

'They would certainly keep you fit if you had to go up and down them every day, huh?' Jaq said, grinning at her partner. 'I'd give an arm and a leg to be able to relocate here, but I probably couldn't afford the rent, despite the lack of a lift.'

'I don't know. It's got to be cheaper than Angel.'

'I wouldn't bet on it. With the Docklands nearby, the rents around here are silly high. Not that I need much. I barely go home to sleep, so I'm fine with a studio, but they're hard to come by and anything bigger is usually out of my price range.'

'Yeah, we should have both gone into finance like all the office workers around us. Then we wouldn't have to worry about having a roof over our heads.'

'I wonder how White does it,' Jaq said. 'Sarah's paid better than me and even she and Aaron can't afford a nice place in this location. They're looking to move right out of London and commute in so that they can afford to buy a house. Simon must be on similar money.'

Darren nodded, but looked too winded by the climb to comment. He was alright though, Jaq thought. He and his wife had bought their little terrace just before the housing boom kicked off.

'Well, here we are,' Jaq said coming to a stop before Simon White's beautifully stripped and varnished wooden door that was quite a contrast to his neighbours' who'd painted their doors everything from black to white, blue and even a pink door further along the balcony.

'This was your idea,' Darren said, tilting his head meaningfully.

So Jaq rang the doorbell. Then the two of them stared at the intercom light, waiting for it to come on. Jaq always counted slowly to ten when she was waiting for a response. She felt that was more than sufficient for a person to get to the door. After that, she rang again when the flat stayed dark and silent. Then she rang a third time, keeping her finger on the bell that little bit longer.

This time, the light came on.

'You again.' Simon's voice sounded electronic and a touch hysterical. 'It's one thirty in the morning. What the hell is going on?'

'Mr White, sorry to bother you so late.' Jaq schooled her voice and face to convey a maximum level of apology. 'We were wondering whether you could help us.'

'I'm not opening the door unless you have a warrant.'

'We're on a time sensitive case and we really could use your help to get through to our two suspects, Simon. Please.'

'Get through?' Simon sounded confused now.

'They're young, fourteen and fifteen, and we think they've abducted a twelve-year-old. We're really worried about his safety.'

'Get a professional to help you. A shrink or... or a social worker.'

'We wouldn't be here if we hadn't already tried everything else. You're our last long shot. Otherwise, in a couple of hours we'll have to let them go and you can bet they won't go anywhere near the kid in case we're tailing them, which we will be.'

There was a long pause, so long, Jaq was tempted to ask again, but Darren shook his head and gestured to wait. To her surprise, a couple of seconds later, Simon opened the door a crack and peered out at them.

'What exactly would you want me to do?'

'Try to talk some sense into them,' Darren said, much to Jaq's relief. She felt like Simon was more angry with her than with Darren, so it was best he took the lead.

'You're closer in age to them, so they'll be able to relate better to you. You've also spent time in a young offenders' institution.'

Simon pulled the door nearly shut, but even so they could see that he'd turned paler.

'My... my juvenile record?'

'Ah! I'm sorry... we didn't tell you last time, did we?' Jaq said. 'It wasn't relevant in the end, but your record was flagged when we were looking into potential suspects.'

'I can't help you,' Simon said, and now the door had only a hair's width crack. 'Please leave.'

'Simon, please.' Jaq said, putting her hand on the door to keep it open without making it look like she was going to force her way in. 'The information will go no further than Darren and I. Please!'

Simon was shaking now, looking as scared as when they'd hauled him in over Liz's disappearance.

'We'll make it as easy as we can for you. Just help us and held Brad.'

'Who?'

'Brad Davis, the missing boy.'

Simon stared blankly at Jaq, then glanced across at Darren, who gave him a wry smile. Jaq wished he'd do more because she didn't feel like she was getting through to Simon.

But to her surprise, he took a deep breath and said, 'So... you want them to be scared straight?'

'It works on some kids,'

'You really think I can do anything your people couldn't do?'

'Honestly, we do not know, but we're willing to give it a go.'

Simon stared at her like she'd lost her mind, then back to Darren.

'You guys really must be desperate. Let me put some clothes on,' he muttered and closed the door in their faces.

'Well, I guess we couldn't expect a warm welcome,' Darren said with a grin.

Less than ten minutes later, Simon reappeared, dressed in jeans and a long-sleeved navy t-shirt with a leather satchel slung across his body.

'What's that?' Jaq asked, already heading back to the stairs.

'My work stuff. I don't know how long you'll need me, but I'm damned if I'm going to be late for work.'

'Fair enough. We can't actually hold them past 6:30 anyway,' Jaq said, and just got a curt nod from Simon.

He looked grim, pale and on edge. Hopefully, the boys wouldn't pick up on his nerves. They were the type who could sniff out weakness and prey on it.

'Do you have some idea of what you might say to them?' Darren asked as they set off down the stairs.

Simon clattered after him, pointedly ignoring Jaq.

'The institute used to get some of the ex-offenders to give us talks. Telling us how hard their lives were because they'd been to prison and warning us not to go down the same path.'

It surprised Jaq that Simon was willing to talk about something he'd clearly wanted to keep a secret. Her experience as an interrogator made her decide he was trying to cover up his fear with chat.

'Did it work? Hearing from reformed prisoners?'

'Maybe.'

'Did it convince you?'

'I had no intention of going into a life of crime.'

Jaq wondered whether that was true. Clever criminals operated for years without being noticed. Simon's father, aside from being a serial killer, had been a surgeon. He was well educated and meticulous, which was what allowed him to keep killing for such a long time.

Simon worked side by side with him, so had been trained for years. After that, they had locked him up with yet more criminals. Young offenders, admittedly, but he'd have learned a lot there too.

'So it had nothing to do with the talks?' Darren said, bringing Jaq back to the conversation.

'I got lucky. Someone spotted that I could draw and got me accepted into an art school. I don't know what I would have done otherwise.'

'Yeah, you did get lucky,' Darren said as they reached the ground floor. 'Opportunity and support probably do more to help young guys go straight than a scary talk about what might happen if they don't. I get that, but at the moment, all we've got is option two.'

'Okay,' Simon said as he climbed into the car. 'So who else will be there? A social worker?'

'And the parents,' Jaq said, buckling herself in as Darren took off at speed.

'What are they like?'

Jaq was glad Simon was asking. At least he was engaging.

'The older boy, Chazza, only has his mum. She's a cleaner and has been giving him hell for getting involved. We had to remove her from the interviews because she was getting physically and verbally abusive to him, us and the social worker.

'The younger boy, Miles, has a very respectable doctor father, who is adamant his son couldn't possibly have done anything wrong. The mother is a stay at home mum who's a bit of a mouse. She's the one sitting in on all the interviews while the father's been on his mobile hunting around for a lawyer. Fortunately, he hasn't had any success so far.'

'Okay,' Simon said, and looked unenthusiastically up at the police station entrance as Darren came to a halt at the front door.

'You go in. I'll park and follow you,' Darren said.

So Jaq led Simon up the stairs, through a foyer filled with the usual drunks from the evening's revelries, some passed out on the chairs before the desk sergeant, two men bellowing football chants, arms over each other's shoulders, while a girl shouted abuse at every person who passed her.

'We're upstairs. It's quieter there,' Jaq said, leading the way to their incident room on the first floor.

She nodded a greeting to the few members of the team collating all the information coming in from the people on the ground. Some hunched over monitors. Others were making phone calls, or filling in the hundreds of forms every case required.

'Here.'

Jaq stopped before the two monitors that displayed feed from the interrogation rooms.

Simon shuddered and said, 'Not there. I can't talk to them there.'

'Where else can you talk to them?' Jaq asked, not entirely surprised by his visceral reaction.

'Anywhere else. Don't you have another room? Somewhere... less intimidating.'

'Oh, okay, we've got a room we use for interviewing victims. It's still got cameras. We'll be recording everything and the social worker will be present, but it fits your criteria.'

Simon was in a daze. This was partly because of the anxiety meds he'd taken to help him sleep but mostly because of the surreal situation. He stepped into an interview suite that was laid out to look like a living room with facing sofas and a low table between them.

The social worker was a thin, older woman who was so tired she was nodding off in the comfortable chair she'd occupied in a corner of the room away from the main group of chairs. At least she wasn't right beside the boy.

He was a big kid, as tall as an average adult male, and chubby, which added to his imposing look. He'd sat down, but then flopped over onto the sofa, his head resting on his arms, half asleep. Simon sat on the opposite sofa, wondering what the hell he should say.

He'd specialised in avoidance at the institute, keeping away from everybody else. Mainly because he'd grown up alone and didn't know how to approach kids his own age, or people in general. He'd also had it hammered into him by his father to never say anything, which was a hard habit to break.

The kids around him had been a scary bunch. Half of them were violent, the other half suicidal. None were good at expressing their feelings with anything other than their fists.

In this, the kid in front of him was familiar, and he supposed after three years locked in with similar boys, he knew something about them. This boy was tough, but exhausted and probably feeling like he was out of options.

Simon opened his case and took out his sketchbook and pencil case and selected one of his soft black pencils. Art therapy would probably not cut it, but he could do some work of his own while he waited. He had an advert concept he needed to prepare, after all.

Simon flicked through to the storyboard he was working on. At least yogurt was an easy product to promote. Most people liked it and considered it healthy.

Chazza sat up, blinking in the bright light of the room and watched. Simon was super aware of him but carried on drawing.

'What are you doing?' Chazza asked.

'My work.'

'What is it?'

'I'm a designer at a media company.'

'So what the fuck are you doing here?' Chazza's voice drawled. Swearing seemed to be a habit because they'd been no emphasis on the word. 'You're in the wrong room.'

'No, I'm in the right room.'

Experience had taught Simon that the best way to treat violent boys was to keep them confused. He flicked back to a piece of earlier work he didn't need, and wrote something on the paper, making sure the angle wasn't readable by the camera. He tore the page out and put it on the table, along with another of his soft pencils. No sense in giving the boy anything sharp he could use as a weapon.

'What the fuck is that?'

'An example of my work, take a look.'

'I don't care about your work.'

'No, but by now you must be bored out of your mind, aren't you?'

'I just want to sleep,' Chazza said, but glanced at the paper. Put it down, then picked it up again and looked a bit more closely.

Simon kept his eyes on his work.

'Do you want to get out of here?'

'I'm going to get out of here. I'm a minor. They can't hold me much longer.'

'Anyone over the age of ten is considered capable of telling right from wrong and is therefore liable for prosecution. They would send you to a young offenders' institution, but that's still a prison, no matter what they call it. Didn't they already tell you that?'

'Didn't believe them,' Chazza muttered.

'Why not?'

'We were told different.'

'Who told you?' Simon asked, keeping his head down, apparently absorbed in his work, although currently all he could focus on was drawing swirls and blobs.

'Some guy.'

'Older?'

Chazza just shrugged and Simon sensed that he's say no more. That he probably suspected he shouldn't have said as much as he already had.

'Do you like your mother?'

'What kind of a fucking question is that?'

'Just wondering whether you'd rather spend time with her than in a young offenders' institution.'

'Oh, so here comes the lecture, huh? Is that what you're here for, to frighten me?'

'Actually,' Simon said, looking Chazza straight in the eye. 'If they had given me the choice, I'd have picked the young offenders' over my father.'

That astonished Chazza, who muttered, 'My mum's a cow.'

Simon just smiled.

'They didn't give me a choice. They sent me to the young offenders'. It was shit, but better than home. That's all I've got to say.'

Simon tilted his head at the paper he'd given Chazza. The kid looked at it for a while, doodled on it briefly and handed it back to Simon.

'Nah, man, they've got nothing on me. I'm not saying anything.'

'Fair enough.'

Simon folded the paper and then waved to the camera. It was the signal for Chazza to be removed. Jaq appeared at the door, looking irritated as she told the social worker to accompany Chazza back to the interrogation room, along with a uniformed police officer.

'Are you even trying?' Jaq asked once the boy was out of earshot.

'What do you want from me?' Simon said, angered by this woman who thought nothing of hauling him out of bed in the middle of the night, then having the cheek to be annoyed. 'Just send in the other boy.'

'We started you off on Chazza because he's the leader. Miles is just a little shit.'

'But he'll also know where the kid is, won't he?'

'Yeah, so try harder this time, okay?'

Simon didn't bother responding, not that Jaq gave him a chance. He just sat down on the sofa again and flipped through his sketchbook, looking for another disposable page. He'd just finished writing his note when a weaselly, skinny kid walked in, accompanied by a similar, worn down looking woman and a large social worker, doing her best to keep alert. The kid looked small for a fourteen-year-old, but cocky and wide awake.

'Who the fuck are you?' Miles said as he threw himself on the sofa, leaning back like a gangster rapper. His mother settled on the sofa, on the far end from her son. She looked like her son intimidated her. That was saying something for a fourteen-year-old.

The boy's arrogant attitude probably came from the father. It was the advantage of well-off parents. Money bought confidence. Much as he hated to admit it, as the son of a doctor himself, he'd come across as arrogant to some of the other boys at the institute, too. He'd always thought that highly ironic.

'Is it entertaining hanging around with the lower classes?' Simon asked, pretty sure that was Miles's aim. That and avoidance of bullies by hanging out with the biggest bully.

Miles gave him a wide grin, cleared his throat and spat on the carpet. He was definitely aiming to shock, but Simon had seen human excrement smeared on the walls in protest and just turned his attention back to his sketchbook.

'You're just a nobody who's been called in because the police are getting desperate, aren't you?'

'Pretty much,' Simon said. 'And you think you're cleverer than the cops, don't you?'

'Phffft, obviously. In about three hours, they're going to have to let us go.'

'It was pretty sloppy of you to have got caught in the first place, and for what? Abducting some kid? '

'You think you could do better?'

'I did do better,' Simon said, looking up to give Miles a cool stare.

The boy's confidence carried the day and his grin merely got wider.

'So... you're just some loser who got caught and is now trying to make me confess to get in good with the cops. That's really pathetic.'

'You got me.' Simon tore a page from his sketchbook and put it down on the table along with a pencil. 'I got done for six murders. Yet here I am, free as a bird, while you're looking at some serious time, especially if you're tried as the instigator.'

'At worst, I'm just an accomplice.'

'Are you? That doesn't get you much protection under English law. Have they not told you about joint enterprise?'

'So you're a lawyer now?'

'I'm a graphic designer,' Simon said, holding his sketchpad up, a design facing Miles.

'You call that art?' Miles said, grabbed the paper on the table and spent some time scrawling on it before he handed it back with a sneer. 'You're just a pathetic loser. Six murders, my arse.'

Simon looked down at the paper Miles gave him, nodded, held out his hand and said, 'Pencil.'

Miles threw it at him, but more because he was caught off guard. Apparently, he'd planned to hold on to the pencil.

'Good luck,' Simon said and left, closing the door behind him with a firm click.

'Is that it?' Jaq said, dashing over from the monitor where she and Darren had been watching the meeting.

'That Miles is a snake. I wouldn't be so sure he wasn't the ring leader.'

'You got that from the five minutes you spent with him, did you? Thanks for bloody nothing, Simon. We've just wasted one hell of a lot of time and got absolutely bugger all for it.'

'I told you I couldn't help.'

'I didn't expect you to put in so little effort. Why did you even bother coming?'

'I told you!'

'It was a total disaster.'

'Fuck you!' Simon said, shoved the papers he was clutching in his hand at Jaq and stormed out.

'Shit, I'm sorry,' Jaq said to Darren, who'd strolled over.

'It's okay, I'm also disappointed.' Darren bent down to pick up the papers Jaq had left on the floor. He unfolded the two sheets, looked at the first, then flicked it over, and looked at the second. 'Hold on,' he murmured. 'Look at this.'

For the second time, Jaq had the papers thrust at her but this time she took them.

'What is it?'

A host of scrawled dicks of the sort teenage boys drew everywhere were the first thing she noticed. Followed by a couple of pencil sketches that seemed to be an advert for a car. Above that was the line, *If you want to get out of this, give me a location.*

The script was so beautiful Jaq didn't register the meaning right away. Then she did a double take before she flicked to the second page. In amongst the pencil sketches for a dieting app was the same beautifully written line. Below that in thick black pencil was a childish scrawl: *Scout hut by the canal.*

Jaq looked up at Darren, who was watching her with one raised eyebrow.

'You don't think that's where Brad Davis is, do you?'

'Only one way to find out.'

'If it is, then I owe Simon a huge apology.'

'Worry about that later,' Darren said as he ran for his desk and picked up a walkie talkie whilst shouting to the rest of the room to find the address of the scout hut and get an ambulance sent to the same location.

7

⸺ ⸱ ⸺

IT'S A NICE EVENING, Simon thought as he made his way upstairs. Home after a work gathering to welcome the new interns. Any excuse for drinks, really.

This time it had been on the deck of a riverside pub and the weather had been perfect. He liked the start of the summer as the evenings began to lengthen. There was a serenity to the sky at twilight that he found particularly restful.

Simon reached the top floor, stepped out of the stairwell and froze. A figure in a dark hoodie lay slumped against his door. He couldn't move, he couldn't breathe. What the hell was this?

Shit, it was a woman! Simon felt the shakes start as he forced himself to approach the figure. Should he call the cops?

It was best not to touch her, right? What if she was dead? What did he do then? For Christ's sake, why did these things keep happening to him lately?

He stopped just out of reach of the body and crouched down, praying that it was just a passed out vagrant or a teenager who'd gone too far on a binge. Safe enough to call an ambulance for someone like that, right?

It was definitely a woman. She had shapely legs in tight jeans and even the hoodie was fitted and zipped all the way up. Her hands were slipped into the front pockets with a black plastic bag, full, by the looks of things, wrapped around one wrist. Long hair fell forward, obscuring her face.

'Um... excuse me?'

'Humph,' the woman muttered and gave a little jerk.

Alive, thank god.

'Look, you can't pass out here.' Simon was trying to work out why she felt familiar. Was she a neighbour? He thought they were all older. Maybe one of their kids. 'You need to go home.' Simon shuffled closer, weighing up whether it was safe to give the girl a shake.

The woman suddenly lifted her head, blowing extravagantly to get rid of the hair. As it fell away from her face, Simon realised with deepening dismay why she felt so familiar.

'Detective Burnham?'

'Simon!' Jaq smiled beatifically at him. 'Simon me old mucker. We solved the case and found the boy, all thanks to you. And I... I owe you an apology. I'd have texted you to let you know but I couldn't.' Jaq let go an impressive burp. 'Can't use police information for personal matters. So I thought I'd come tell you in person. Brought some fried chicken and chips, and a couple of beers by way of apology and 'cus you need fattening up.'

'Shhh, keep your voice down,' Simon said, wondering how to get this drunk woman home. It would be next to impossible to get her safely back to ground level in her current state. He was convinced she must have crawled up the stairs.

'Let's eat.' Jaq scrabbled at the door in an ineffectual attempt to get back onto her feet.

Simon stared down at her, trying to work out what he did.

'Where's your partner?'

'Drunk as a skunk. Got him a cab and sent him home.'

'I see.'

Simon looked up and down the balcony, trying to think of other options. He doubted an ambulance would come and pick her up. They were more likely to tell him off for wasting their time.

Likewise, calling the local station would also get him a ticking off and D.I Burnham probably wouldn't want to look bad in front of her colleagues. But if that was the case, why get this blind drunk?

'I shouldn't have yelled at you,' Jaq said. 'I'm really, really, really sorry. I'm usually better than that but tiredness and... Nope, no, all just an excuse. I'm just sorry.'

Weirdly enough, getting an apology, even from somebody who was so drunk she probably wouldn't remember doing it the next day, still made him feel better. He'd seen the news, of course. He knew the boy had been found and rushed to the hospital. So Simon hadn't needed more.

He wondered what he'd have done if they hadn't gone to the scout hut. Would he have gone back to the station and told them? He shrugged the thought away. It was irrelevant now, and he had a more pressing problem.

There really only seemed to be one option. He unlocked his door and eased it open. Jaq slipped down it onto her back, half in and half out of the house. Then he stepped over her, took a deep breath to prepare himself both mentally and physically, grabbed the detective under her arms and pulled her inside.

Fortunately, there was very little friction over the wooden floor. It was just when he reached the living room carpet that he struggled.

'Are we not going to eat?' Jaq asked, waving her plastic bag.

The smell of chicken and chips was surprisingly appealing, even though Simon had eaten a reasonable burger at the pub.

'You are going to sleep.'

Simon rolled the detective onto the carpet and decided that was far enough. He fetched a cushion, put it under her head, eased the bag of food off her wrist, and covered her with a green fleecy blanket.

'Sleep,' Jaq muttered, her eyes already shut. 'I remember that. I like sleep.'

'Yeah, good.' Simon gave the woman a reassuring pat on her shoulder. 'Sweet dreams then.'

All the exercise left him breathless and he dropped onto a dining chair, still huffing as he watched the detective. She was out cold, which was confirmed a few seconds later by a snort, and then a rhythmic, light snoring.

Simon rummaged in the bag, removing the two cans of lager that were oily and gritty with the salt from the chips that had spilled out of their box. He opened a can with a satisfying hiss and hastily sucked up the frothing foam. Then he fished a chicken leg out of the other box and bit into it, all while watching D.I. Burnham.

Why had she come? Was it really just to apologise? He'd never been alone with anyone in his house before and certainly not a woman, an unconscious woman. That thought made his hand shake so violently he dropped the chicken and looked around, checking his cameras.

Then he looked back at Jaq Burnham. She was very attractive. She'd also been impressive at the police station. Very no-nonsense, including to him, but he brushed that aside.

It was sheer madness to have her here. A woman passed out on the floor was all too familiar and terrifying. It reminded him of other women, dead women, and his father. He ran to his room and locked the door, taking deep breaths to try to calm himself.

Once he could breathe more evenly, he went to bed. He was used to staring up at a darkened ceiling for hours at a time, and tonight was no different. But he couldn't stay there. Not with an unconscious woman in the other room. What if she threw up and then choked to death?

So he got up and went back to the sitting room and watched the slow rise and fall of Jaq's chest. It was so disturbing he decided it would be better if he left. He grabbed his house keys and headed outside.

He could walk around the block where the CCTV would pick him up. That way, if anything happened, he'd at least be recorded as outside. But how long would he do that for? Wouldn't it look suspicious if he was on camera going round and round for hours on end when he knew Jaq was in his house?

He was halfway down the stairs when he decided that wasn't a viable option, either. So he trudged back up. The best thing to do was to keep his distance, but make sure his home camera filmed everything.

He sat with his back to Jaq and tried to ignore her presence by watching a Netflix show on his iPad, but he couldn't focus. It was going to be a very long night.

A truly dreadful headache, accompanied by a furry, foul tasting tongue, woke Jaq. She forced herself to open her eyes and stared at a collection of legs of the table and chair variety. She rolled over and bumped into a coffee table, then lay staring at a sunny ceiling. Tilting her head over to the other side, she noted a white chiffon curtain billowing in a light breeze coming from the open windows above her.

'Shit,' Jaq said out loud, and sat bolt upright. 'Shit, shit, shit,' she added as the sudden movement ten times-ed her headache.

She was at Simon White's house! On the floor, but fully clothed, thank God, and covered with an olive green fleece. How drunk had she got?

Sure, they'd all been elated when Brad Davis had finally woken up and identified his two kidnappers and they'd hauled the two boys in now with plenty of evidence against them. They'd drunk too much in celebration and the rest was a hazy mess.

But to turn up here? She'd meant to apologise to Simon, of course. He'd played a crucial part. But she'd meant to turn up at a civilised hour and be suitably humble. She wasn't even sure what she'd said to him.

How stupid to pass out in the house of a man who'd been involved with a serial killer, too. Jaq shuddered at the very idea. It was stupid to get so drunk in the first place, but that was the police for you. They never did anything in half measures and finding a missing boy alive... well. But this, passing out in the house of a man she didn't trust. What had possessed her?

'Arg, water,' she muttered and clambered to her feet, blinking as the headache throbbed.

She put her mouth to the tap and chugged all she could, then she looked around again. Her bag was in the middle of the dining room table, a yellow post-it on top, a box of paracetamol next to it.

'Bless you!' Jaq said to the house in general. Then she swooped on the painkillers, popped a pair of pills and this time got out a glass for the water.

Then she read the note.

I hope you feel okay. Thanks for the chicken, beer and apology.

The washing machine does a half load in thirty minutes, plus another 30 to dry. There's a spare toothbrush in the bathroom. Use the towel with the yellow border in the bathroom. It is also the only place in the house without a camera. Please leave the keys in the letterbox when you go.

Cameras all around. Yeah, she'd forgotten about that. Thanks for the warning. Jaq wondered, yet again, what the surveillance was about. And she wondered about the note. Short and to the point, no signature or anything to indicate he'd like to see her again.

Funny thought. Did she want to see him again? He was too thin, too highly strung and with an unpleasant past that a copper couldn't like. All the same, a hi and a signed off name wouldn't have been too much to ask, would it?

Her phone gave a discreet buzz. A text from Darren: *Where are you?*

On my way, she typed as she flicked the kettle on. *Be there in about an hour.*

That would give her sufficient time for a shower, to wash her clothes, and have a decent cuppa. Thank God there was milk in the fridge, that, a half tub of butter and last night's chicken, mostly untouched. The man definitely wasn't eating enough.

Now for the washing machine. Jaq wondered whether she smelled and that was why Simon had mentioned it. She sniffed an armpit. Yep, a shower was in order.

———

'Are you alright, Simon?' Sarah said, bending over to get her face into his field of view.

Simon gave a start as he came back to a sense of where he was and looked around. There was a group of smokers at the back door but far enough away that he could only hear a murmur of voices. Fortunately, the wind was also blowing away from them so his lunch, a barely touched BLT from Pret, didn't smell of smoke.

'Yeah, I'm fine.'

'Mind if I join you, then?'

Simon wasn't thrilled but shifted along the bench the office had put out in the small green space at the back of the building and gave a slight nod.

'How's your prep going for your week in charge?' Sarah asked.

'Fine. There isn't much to do since you've worked so hard to wrap things up before you go away.'

'And the team? I get the feeling they're looking forward to you being in charge. Don't let them give you any problems.'

'They're all grownups and more than capable of looking after themselves.'

'What about the interns? Liz said they're already following you around.'

'Yeah,' Simon said and ran his fingers through his hair. He was too tired for a conversation, but the situation with the interns was stranger than usual. He always had some contact with interns and was happy to teach any newbies the ropes, but these two were especially enthusiastic. 'Aisha asks me a hundred questions a day and Brian seems to think I need constant coffee refills.'

Sarah laughed and said, 'Lucky you.'

'Why?'

'Aisha told me that your work is amazing. She's determined to learn as much as she can from you while she's here. You should feel flattered.'

'And Brian?'

'Well... Brian's gay.'

Simon was definitely too tired to interpret Sarah's amused smile and just shrugged.

'Everyone in the office thinks he fancies you and as you are sexually ambiguous, I guess he decided it's worth a try.'

'I'm sexually ambiguous?'

'Nobody knows whether you prefer men or women or even whether you're asexual.'

'Is that an actual topic of conversation?' Simon asked, not knowing what to do with the information.

'Don't worry, we don't go on and on about it. But as you've never had a partner and you're a good-looking guy, people have talked.'

'Oh.'

Simon wondered whether people's curiosity was worth getting upset about.

'Are you okay? You've been looking spaced out all morning.'

'I had a weird night.' Simon couldn't think how else to explain. 'Your friend Jaq showed up drunk and landed up sleeping on my floor.' The moment the words were out, Simon wished he could take them back, but it was too late. 'Does she do that kind of thing often?'

'Jaq? Never as far as I'm aware. She must really trust you.'

Simon highly doubted that but thought it best not to say so. Otherwise he'd have to explain, and that was impossible, not without revealing that he had a criminal past.

'But why would she even go to your flat?' Sarah asked.

Simon regretted having brought the subject up, because to explain he'd have to tell her about his past. This was something he'd never do.

'I don't know. I'm close to the police station, I guess.'

'So you didn't ask her?'

'She wasn't exactly sober when she arrived, and I had to leave for work before she woke up. All I can tell you is she was muttering sorry, sorry,' Simon said and waved his hand in dismissal.

Sarah, though, appeared to be fascinated.

'Maybe she felt bad about hauling you in when Liz vanished. Jaq's terrible at admitting when she's at fault.

The alcohol probably helped her screw up the courage to see you.'

Simon gave her an awkward shrug come grimace, praying she didn't ask him more.

'Does Jaq have a boyfriend?'

The question escaped him when it was still half-formed. Maybe he needed to know in case Jaq turned up drunk again, so he had somebody to call. Sarah misunderstood and swivelled on the bench to face him properly, a conspiratorial smile creasing her face.

'Why? Do you fancy her?'

'No, of course not. I just...' What could he say?

'She doesn't, but not for lack of trying. Actually, never mind that,' Sarah said, flapping her hands in dismissal. 'Now that I think about it, you two could be good together.'

'No, I really don't think—'

'She comes over as abrupt and very direct and she doesn't suffer fools gladly, but she's a great woman. You couldn't find any better,' Sarah said, ignoring Simon's shaking head. 'She saved my life when we were at school, nothing dramatic. I knocked myself out diving into the pool. If she hadn't noticed and rescued me, I probably would have drowned. And you've already met her a couple of times, so you're halfway there on the getting to know you front.'

'She arrested me,' Simon said.

Sarah laughed.

'Wouldn't that be the perfect thing to tell your kids when they ask how the two of you met?'

'No, really, I don't think she likes me at all.'

'That's just her brusqueness getting in the way of her love life again. Seriously, give her a chance.'

Simon just blinked at Sarah, overwhelmed by her enthusiasm. He'd never considered getting a girlfriend. It was too fraught a subject entangled with hideous memories, his own burning desires and paralysing fears. It was never going to happen with anyone, but especially not a cop who knew too much about him.

'Think about it,' Sarah said, gave Simon a wave and went back inside.

Simon stared at his half-eaten sandwich, sighed and slid it back into its cardboard container. He eased the fiddly plastic lid back on and returned to his desk.

'Coffee, boss!' Brian said seconds later and slid a full mug into Simon's view.

Until today, Simon had merely nodded his thanks and kept working. Today he leaned back in his seat and looked up at the rosy faced boy with the wavy brown hair and sincere blue eyes. He supposed he looked... star-struck, maybe bashful?

'Umm... Brian... I'm not gay,' Simon said and regretted the words the moment he'd uttered them as Brian's expression turned from astonished to embarrassed. 'I mean... it's fine. I'm... I just don't want you to waste your time.'

'Understood,' Brian said, his cheeks growing redder. 'But if you don't mind, I'll just carry on as before.'

'Okay.' This was unfamiliar territory for Simon, who supposed he'd been naïve to assume his sexuality and hangups were his own business. 'You do make excellent coffee.'

8

—◦—

'YOU LOOK FABULOUS,' SARAH said as she gave Jaq an appraising stare while the two of them stood in front of a full-length mirror.

'The only one who looks fab here is you,' Jaq said, adjusting the folds on Sarah's lacy ivory wedding veil. 'Which is as it should be. Nobody should outshine the bride.'

'Quite right!' Sarah gave her trademark cheeky smile that crinkled her nose charmingly and that didn't quite go with her elegant bride's makeup.

'All the same, this dress...' Jaq murmured, as Sarah was called away to do the finishing touches to her makeup.

It was a lilac bridesmaid dress with far too many frills, ribbons and lace that had cost a small fortune. Jaq hadn't minded. Sarah was her best friend, after all. Even though she would never wear the dress again and she looked like she'd escaped from a Victorian melodrama, it was a fair trade.

Jaq's personal style tended to be figure hugging with minimal ornamentation or even patterns. At most, she might opt for some layering. At the moment, she felt like a gangly sugar plum fairy.

There was no time to worry about that though, as there seemed to be a hundred and one things still to be done for the wedding. Since neither Sarah nor Aaron were religious, they'd opted for a humanist wedding and blown their budget on a fancy country manor hotel, so at least most things were being managed by the hotel staff. Still, there were requests and queries from friends and hotel staff alike and it was Jaq's role to deal with as many as possible to ensure Sarah's day passed with minimal stress.

'I hardly slept a wink last night,' Sarah said as she headed for the door that opened into the hotel ballroom and stood fidgeting with her bouquet.

'It doesn't show. You look radiant,' Jaq said.

'Do you have the ring?'

'Of course.' Jaq held the small red velvet box out for inspection. 'It will be fine.'

Which was what she'd been saying since the hen night party the weekend before and she was right. Sarah's dad walked her down the aisle looking very proud. The service was lovely, the reception speeches were short and humorous and the food was delicious.

Then, just before the music struck up for the dancing, Sarah threw her bouquet out into the crowd. It flew straight towards Jaq, who had no choice but to catch it if she didn't want to be hit in the face.

'You did that deliberately,' Jaq said when Sarah returned to the top table after her opening waltz with Aaron.

'Of course I did,' Sarah said with her disarming laugh. 'How is your romantic life progressing?'

'It's going absolutely nowhere,' Jaq said with an expressive sigh. 'Rob asked me out on a date and I told him I'd have to take a rain check as I was working.'

'Does he know what you do yet?'

'Not yet, but he's getting progressively more inquisitive. I think I'm going to have to blow him off. I deliberately didn't agree to be his date today because I said I had too much to do for you, but he's asked me for the first dance.'

'You can at least give him that. I thought the two of you got on pretty well at our double date.'

'Superficially, yes. I'm pretty good at being blokey. It's essential with my work colleagues.'

'You're too picky.'

'I thought you weren't so keen on him.'

'Yes... no... I just thought it would be nice if we could go on foursomes again. It was fun.'

'Anyway, you also accuse me of being too intimidating.'

'You're very straightforward. You call bullshit the moment you spot it, and unfortunately Rob is rather prolific when it comes to talking nonsense. And your career has only accentuated that trait of yours. Sometimes, when I've overheard you making small talk with a man, it sounds too much like a police interrogation. Who would want that?'

'Well, I will not change just to get a man. It would feel phoney.'

'Just tone it down for the first couple of dates. Once you decide you like a guy and he likes you, you could show your assertive side.'

'That's too dishonest, and I'm not a great actor. I doubt I'd pull off. I'm just going to have to accept that I'll always be single.'

'Nonsense, you're not a quitter and we have plenty of good looking single guys here today, so get out there and mingle.'

'Who am I to disobey such an order?' Jaq said and since her duties as the Maid-of-Honour were now discharged, she spent a pleasant couple of hours dancing with whoever came up to her, Rob included, but she made a point of not giving him the idea he had exclusive rights to her.

It was easy enough to find dance partners. Men were drawn to her looks. It was her personality that put them off.

As the night progressed, she felt increasingly uncomfortable in the hideous lavender dress and decided she'd done enough and could get changed. So she pushed her way through the cheerfully chatting crowd and out into the quieter hotel foyer. It was considerably cooler out here and as the door closed, the sound of music and chatter became muted and she felt herself relax.

She took a deep breath and looked about. On the far side of the room, she spotted a man facing the notice board, his finger tracing along a line of text as he silently mouthed the words. He looked rather dashing in a dark grey suit, and she decided he was worth a punt. Then she got closer and realised it was Simon White.

They had set aside a couple of tables at the reception for Sarah and Aaron's work friends, but it surprised her that Simon had shown up. Then again, Sarah had said he came to group events.

Since she had to cross the hall to get to her room and she couldn't pretend not to have seen someone she'd been making a beeline towards only seconds before she walked up to him and said, 'Hello, Simon.'

He jumped and spun around and his eyes widened as he realised who was speaking.

'D...D.I—'

'Jaq, just call me Jaq. I'd appreciate if you don't tell everybody what I do for a living.'

'Oh... sure.'

Simon's eyes darted left and right, apparently assimilating the fact that they were alone, aside from the pair working at the hotel reception desk.

'What were you reading?' Jaq asked, because she couldn't actually think of anything else to say.

'It's the itinerary for the wedding.'

'Ah... working out what to do next, huh?'

'Actually... when to go home.'

'You aren't staying over?'

One of the perks of having the wedding at a hotel was that the guests could stay up as late as they liked and drink as much as they wanted without having to worry about driving home.

'I'm getting a lift back with Liz.' Simon froze at the mention of her name, then he hurried on, 'Liz and her boyfriend, since he lives near me.'

'Oh, well, that's handy.'

Simon clasped his right wrist with his left hand. It didn't completely still the tremors and made Jaq feel guilty that Simon was so uncomfortable in her presence. Suspicion of why he might be so jumpy followed immediately after.

Simon nodded, apparently also at a loss for what else to say.

'I'm going to change out of this dress,' Jaq said, by way of taking her leave, then added, 'God only knows what Sarah was thinking, putting us in these hideous things. And she calls herself a designer.'

To her surprise, Simon said, 'It was probably deliberate.'

'What? Deliberate? Why?'

'People are drawn to beauty. Making all of you bridesmaids look frumpy, accentuated her beauty and drew everybody's eyes to her.'

'The cunning little so and so.' Jaq was impressed by Sarah's ingenuity and Simon's perception. 'I suppose it takes a designer to understand what another designer is doing. If I ever get married, I'm going to make Sarah wear the frumpiest dress I can find. It would only be fair.'

Simon blinked at her, apparently at a loss for something to say, when the ballroom doors swung open with a bang. Loud music and the roar of a cheerful crowd filled the room and Rob stalked out, holding a bottle of champagne by the neck.

'There you are,' he said grinning, 'playing hard to get!'

'I was going to change my dress,' Jaq said.

'I can come with and help you,' Rob said, grinning and leaning forward, much too close.

Jaq noted a quiver of disgust flicker across Simon's face and disappear. She wondered what exactly it was that had repulsed him.

'Who's this?' Rob said, just noticing that Jaq wasn't alone. 'Huh? Simon!'

'Hi Rob,' Simon said and now he looked quite calm, neutral and at ease.

'Our genius designer,' Rob said, throwing his arm around Simon's shoulders. 'This man makes it so easy to sign up customers. He's made me a fortune,' Rob said, sinking his voice to a conspiratorial whisper as he winked at Jaq.

'Then maybe you should share your commission,' Simon said as he removed Rob's tightly wrapped arm.

Rob laughed as if he'd just heard a hilarious joke.

'Perks of the job, my friend. You want in you'd have to join Sales.'

'Who would do your designing for you then?'

Jaq watched the exchange with interest. Simon was a different person around Rob. More at ease than when it was just the two of them and, weirdly, it felt like he had the upper hand. This bigger, beefier, more outwardly self assured, apparently higher earning man seemed less significant compared to his quiet counterpart.

'I'd better go back to the party and see if I can find Liz and her boyfriend,' Simon said, giving Jaq and Rob a nod of farewell.

'I'll stay and keep Jaq company,' Rob said, unfortunately remembering what she planned to do and apparently set on following her to her room.

'No, you go back to the party too,' Jaq said, holding up her hand in a blocking sign that the police always used to stop people in their track, along with an absolutely commanding tone to her voice.

Rob wasn't drunk, but certainly heading that way fast. He took a swig from the champagne bottle, wiped his mouth and grinned at Jaq.

'Okay, I'll be waiting. You at least owe me another dance.'

Jaq nodded, noting that Simon was still there, and didn't move as Rob made his way back to the ballroom singing along at the top of his lungs to the pop song that was blaring out.

'Is there something you wanted to say?' Jaq asked, because Simon was back to looking dubious.

Was she really that uncomfortable for him?

'That case,' Simon said, checking nobody was close enough to hear. It would have been hard to do so, because Rob hadn't bothered to close the doors on his way back to the party.

'The missing boy?'

'Yeah.'

'What about it?'

'You probably already picked up on it, but it's been bothering me,' Simon said, his voice dropping so low that Jaq could barely hear him over the noise.

'What's been bothering you?' Jaq asked, which made Simon give a start and step back.

'That kid, Gazza... he gave me the impression, just for a moment, that there was somebody else behind what they did.'

Jaq hadn't picked up on anything like that, and she felt a tingle of alarm. Whether it was because of the case or Simon, she couldn't tell.

'What gave you that idea?'

'Didn't you record the meeting I had with him?'

'We did, of course,' Jaq said, guiltily aware she'd watched the recording over and over again to see what she made of Simon, rather than thinking about what Gazza had said.

'Maybe watch it again,' Simon said, nodded and hurried away.

Jaq contemplated grabbing him and making him explain, but now wasn't the right time. So she filed it into her to do list and went to get changed.

9

A COUPLE OF ROUTINE weeks made Simon feel that life was finally getting back to normal. He'd even stopped taking the sedatives Dr Nobel had prescribed when his doorbell went off in a single sustained burst. It sent a shock wave of fright through him and he glanced up at his kitchen clock: 8 pm.

His hands started shaking in anticipation and it got worse as he checked the entry phone and saw D.I. Burnham at the door. What the hell did she want?

'Yes?'

Simon examined her flickering image like a hawk. She looked like she was alone.

'Sorry to bother you so late, but I came to apologise. Properly this time.'

'No helping the police with their enquiries again?'

Simon was getting jumpier. What if the rest of the police mob was just waiting around the corner?

'I'm here in a private capacity. Well, partly work related, since I'm apologising for my behaviour as a detective. But also—'

Simon didn't want what Jaq was saying to be overheard by the neighbours, so he opened the door.

'Thank you.' Jaq flashed him a terrifyingly friendly smile as she stepped into his flat. She held up a black plastic bag and said, 'I brought food and drink by way of payment.'

'I just lost my appetite,' Simon said as he trailed reluctantly along behind Jaq.

She put the bag of food on his dining room table and made for the kitchen, where she rummaged about for plates, cutlery and a couple of pint glasses.

'Perfect,' she said as she unslung her bag, hooked it on the chair next to her and sat down. 'Do you like curry, Simon?' He nodded, which got him another beaming smile. 'You can't go wrong with a curry, can you? I got something medium hot as I wasn't sure what you can handle.'

Simon felt like his life had turned surreal. He'd never had a visitor. Not once in the five years he'd lived in this flat and now this woman was here for a second time. On top of that, he'd never had a meal with just one other person in his entire adult life.

He'd been super careful not to, especially with a woman. Come to think of it, all his care had come to nothing just because somebody he knew had vanished. It made him jumpy.

'What... what do you want?' he asked as he sat down opposite Jaq.

Jaq eased the covers off the three aluminium foil containers, releasing the scent of curry and basmati rice into the flat.

'Ah yes, that. Sorry, I haven't eaten in days and now I'm starving.'

'You haven't eaten in days? Why not?'

'Another big case. The joys of being in a serious crimes division in a big city. We've just wrapped everything up,' Jaq said, emptying exactly half of the rice onto her plate, and then putting a couple of large spoonfuls of the two curries on either side. One was a rich red, the other a creamy yellow. 'Do you want to hear about the case?'

'Your case?' Simon felt like the night was getting more and more peculiar, but not in a good way. 'Why would you tell me?'

'I don't know,' Jaq said with a sigh as she took a massive mouthful of curry and rice. 'Maybe because you'd understand. Usually I go home to my empty flat and have nobody to decompress to. Not that my colleagues with partners can say much to their other halves, either. There's confidentiality, legal requirements and—'

'If there's confidentiality and legal requirements, then you shouldn't be saying anything to me, anyway.'

'I have to be careful, yes, but there are some things I can say, like I'm feeling shitty, or it's been very stressful. And I can talk about what's already in the public record. That's when not burdening your loved ones with horrors they're better off not hearing about comes into play. Even so, somebody to have a little cry with occasionally would be nice.'

'A little cry?'

Simon was trying to understand what on earth this had to do with him? Maybe Sarah had been encouraging Jaq to get together with him, too.

'I really, really don't want to know about your work.'

'Why not?' Jaq said, giving Simon her coldest police interrogator stare.

At least, that was how it felt to him.

'It's... triggering,' he said and hoped he could leave it at that.

Jaq stared at him for a moment, considering.

'Ok, fair enough, I can understand that. It isn't all fun and games after all.'

Now that Simon looked at Jaq properly, she was grey with exhaustion with dark smudges under her eyes. For the first time, he felt bad for her.

'Maybe you should change jobs.'

'Then who would catch the bad guys?' Jaq gave a tired smile, that was somehow vulnerable and unnerved Simon even more. 'Anyway, that's not why I'm here.'

'You said you came to apologise, but you've already done that.'

'Ah, yeah, I owe you an apology for the apology, too. I don't know what I was thinking showing up rat-arsed. Sarah said you were really uncomfortable about it, which was the last thing I intended. I am sorry. Hence the proper sober apology now. I'd have done it sooner, but what with the wedding and that new case, I've not had a free moment.'

'It's alright.'

Simon finally helped himself to some food. The intense smell had made his mouth water, even though he didn't feel like eating. Spooning the rice and curry onto his plate gave him something to do, though.

'Try the naan bread. It's delicious,' Jaq said as she tore a strip of naan apart with her fingers, dipped it in the red curry and popped it into her mouth. 'I know you don't want to talk about work, but can I ask you a couple of things about those two boys, Chazza and Miles?'

'Okay,' Simon said, wondering whether Jaq had looked into the thing he'd mentioned at the wedding.

'Why did you write the question down on paper? Why didn't you just ask them to tell you where Brad Davis was?'

Ah, a more basic question than he'd expected but an easy enough one to answer.

'You'd been asking them the same thing all day, hadn't you?'

'Of course, and it didn't work, which was why we landed up begging you for help.'

'So if I'd asked them in the same way, they'd have told me the same thing they'd been saying to you. In fact, Miles did, drawing those dicks all over the paper.'

'Yeah, he's a proper little shit, that one. But Chazza told you.'

Simon nodded and ran his fork through the rice, sectioning off a mouthful sized portion.

'I changed the medium.'

'Huh?'

'I do it with our clients sometimes. When we land up going round and round a brief and we can't find common ground, I change the way we're working to get a different solution. Usually we've been talking and putting down bullet points, so I break out the coloured pencils and ask them to draw what they want, or I give them some clay and let them play with it while we talk. It sometimes breaks down a mental barrier and helps people see a new perspective.'

'And that's what you tried with the kids.'

'I also told Chazza he had a choice, to stay with his mum or get away from her. I didn't know which he would take.'

'Seems he thought she was the better option.'

'Although they'll land up being tried now that you know what they did to Brad, won't they?'

'Most likely. He was beaten so badly he was put in a coma, and they'd tied him up in the scout hut, so he couldn't have got away. It was brutal. I think you were right about Miles, too. He's a tricky little so and so.'

Simon nodded and pushed the rice he'd sectioned off into his pool of yellow curry and started blending it.

'Then my second question,' Jaq said, tearing off another strip of naan. 'That thing Gazza said about being told he'd be okay as a minor... Was that what made you think somebody else was involved?'

So finally they'd come to it and he sighed, wishing he'd not said anything at all. Why did he get involved or even spend a second of his time, even considering it?

'It was probably nothing. Just a gut feeling from the way the kid spoke.'

'How he spoke, not what he said?'

'He seemed frightened, but only for a second before he went back to pretending all was okay.'

Jaq nodded, looking thoughtful, which surprised Simon. He'd expected to be dismissed out of hand. After all, his vague suspicion was hardly worth mentioning.

'It isn't what you want to talk about, is it?' Jaq said. 'Me neither, really. So let's change the subject. Are you going anywhere nice for your holidays?'

Simon's first instinct was to tell Jaq that it was none of her business. It felt like she was trying to dig information out of him. Then he remembered that people's number one topic of conversational at the office was their up coming summer holidays.

'I haven't made any plans yet. I usually take a break after the schools go back.'

'Ah yes, the pleasures of not having to plan holidays around kids,' Jaq said. 'It's one of the few benefits of being single and child free.'

She was watching him now with the universal expression Simon had learned indicated that she'd actually only asked about his holiday so she could talk about hers. He'd been terrible at conversation when he'd finally made it into the outside world, but he'd at least learned that when people asked this kind of question, it was polite to reciprocate.

'What are you planning for your holidays?'

The beaming smile Jaq gave him informed Simon that he'd been right.

'Assuming we don't have a case drop into our laps, I'm going to Cornwall. I can't wait. It will just be me and my sis—'

Jaq stopped so abruptly it made Simon look up from the contemplation of the mess of blended curries and rice he'd made on his plate.

'Sorry,' Jaq said, flashing him an embarrassed smile. 'I tend to be careful about what I tell people about my family, what with being a detective. The fewer people who know about them, the better.'

'That's okay, you don't have to tell me.'

Simon wasn't that keen to know, really. It might make Jaq think he was more interested than he actually was.

'Well, I know all about you, even the bits you want hidden, so I suppose it's okay. And you've probably guessed already, anyway. I'm going on holiday with my sister. In the past, I'd have gone on holiday with Sarah, but that's not really going to be possible anymore. Not unless I can convince her to take a couple of short weekend breaks. But it won't be the same. Do you go on holiday with other people?'

'No.'

'Group holidays?'

'Not that either.'

'So you go on holiday on your own?'

This was becoming too intrusive and Simon was reluctant to say more.

'I usually just stay home and paint.'

Jaq's expression was the same as he used to get from his colleagues, so nowadays he lied to them about his holidays.

'Jesus. Do you have any friends at all?'

'Are you feeling sorry for me?' Simon said and his chest constricted with gathering anger. 'Because you don't need to be. I'm perfectly content with my life.'

'All the same... no man's an island and all that.'

'I am happier now than I have ever been,' Simon said, and it was the truth.

'Have you ever even left London?'

'I went to Sarah's wedding.'

'Oh, and that was so far. A two-hour drive into darkest Kent,' Jaq said with heavy sarcasm. 'Have you ever left the country? Or even, wow, do you even have a passport?'

Simon didn't, but he was damned if he'd say so.

'Tell me more about your family,' he said with a challenge in his eye. 'Do you have any other siblings?'

The advantage of talking to a cop was that they were good at reading people, so now Jaq accepted that she'd pushed him too far.

'Aside from my sister, the lawyer, I have a younger brother who's a musician. My mom's a teaching assistant and my dad's a car salesman. We were all born and brought up in Croydon and my parents still live there.'

Jaq tilted her head as if to say, there you are, anything else?

'Oh,' was all Simon could come up with.

So he took a larger than intended mouthful of curry and chewed it meditatively as he dropped his gaze to the container of bright red sauce covering lumps of tandoori chicken.

'Sorry, again. I really didn't come to fight.' Jaq heaved a tremendous sigh, stretched her arms above her and looked around blearily. 'I don't suppose you've got a spare bedroom, have you?'

'What? No.' Was this woman seriously inviting herself over? Her brass neck astonished Simon.

'Sorry, just kidding,' Jaq said. 'I would never do that. Although, at times like this when my body feels like a lump of lead, I wish teleportation existed and someone could zap me home in an instant.'

'Just finish your food and go.'

Simon jumped up and started tidying away the dishes and the remains of the food. He was aware that Jaq was watching him, but too worried about what she might say next to look at her. Instead, he took all the dishes to the sink and started washing up, which kept his back to her. All the while he prayed Jaq would take the hint. But there was no sound of a chair being pushed back or anything else to indicate that she had left.

Finally, he'd done all he could and turned around, steeling himself to tell Jaq to bugger off. But his resolve and rehearsed words evaporated. She'd fallen asleep, her head resting on her arms that were draped over the dining room table.

'Shit,' Simon muttered. 'This again.'

So he fetched the fleece he'd used on her last time, draped it over Jaq's shoulders and went to his room. It was going to be another sleepless night. Simon double checked that his surveillance system was working. He closed the door to his room and contemplated locking it but didn't. She was already inside his house, after all. Then he lay on his bed, flipped open his iPad, launched Netflix, and started on a new box set.

Her stiff neck finally became so uncomfortable that Jaq opened her eyes to discover that she'd fallen asleep at the dining room table. God, this would require another apology. She hadn't meant to do it since it was clear Simon had been uncomfortable with her presence.

Simon had left a light on and she looked up at the clock. It was one in the morning. It was too late to catch the tube and she couldn't face tracking down a night bus, nor did she want the expense of a taxi, especially when just getting her ass off this chair felt like too much effort.

She looked around blearily, spotted the sofa and stood up and the fleece, that she hadn't noticed draped about her shoulders, fell to the floor. Simon again. He was surprisingly considerate for somebody who wasn't thrilled to have her around. It had hurt when he'd told her to go home. Ah well, time enough to think about that later.

For now, Jaq retrieved the fleece, trundled over to the sofa, kicked off her shoes, plumped one cushion while sweeping the rest onto the floor, curled into a foetal position and went back to sleep.

Jaq slept longer than she'd intended but woke feeling stiff, mashed into the upright of the sofa. She rolled around to find the sun shining into a vaguely familiar room. It was amazing how, with the light pouring through a floor to ceiling window softened by a diaphanous white curtains, the whole place looked very different.

She wondered where she'd put her bag so she could check her phone, then realised she could see the clock from here too. It was just past nine thirty. Damn, but she must have been tired. She wasn't particularly comfortable now either. Mid-century furniture might be elegant, but it didn't have much padding.

Jaq groaned as she pushed herself up and then stretched to work out the kinks in her body. As she did so, she noticed the easel on the opposite side of the room with a large canvas propped up on it. She strolled over and discovered it was a half-finished rendition of a towering cumulonimbus cloud. So Simon was the one who'd painted all the sky pictures hanging on the walls, huh? He had talent.

Where was he, though? The bedroom door was shut, but considering the hour... Then again, it was Saturday, so maybe he was in bed. Jaq tapped on the door but got no response. Either he was asleep, or he was avoiding her, or he'd gone out. Did it matter which was correct?

She considered opening the door, but decided against it. She had a feeling he wouldn't hide in his room. He'd been pretty up front about telling her to go home. He was more likely to come out and hurry her away than wait for her to leave. Ah well, hopefully he had all she required for a cup of tea in that spartan kitchen of his. Then she'd get out of his hair.

She made her way over to the kitchen and spotted a bright yellow post-it note attached to her bag lying centred on the dining room table.

You can have the curry if you want breakfast, the note read in Simon's extraordinarily neat cursive. *Please return the house key as you did last time.*

Simon

Well, he'd signed it. Jaq supposed that was progress. Progress? Why did she want progress? From this man who she couldn't quite trust. Then again, for someone she didn't trust, she'd been oddly willing to sleep at his place. If he was dangerous, it was a foolish thing to do. So why had she done it twice already?

This was a question that she needed to discuss with a friend. Sarah, perhaps? She fished out her phone and sent a text.

Do you fancy brunch, or is wedded bliss going to keep you from me?

Seconds later, her phone pinged.

I'm already a rugby widow. Brunch sounds perfect.

'Rugby widow?' Jaq said as Sarah wove her way past several outdoor tables of the park cafe to where Jaq had snagged their favourite spot. It provided shade for her from a nearby tree, and sun for Sarah. It was the way they liked it.

'Aaron's at his rugby club as we speak. Apparently the boys can't do without him, especially as he missed the week of our honeymoon.'

'I thought rugby was a winter sport.'

'Apparently it's a year round thing for the amateurs. A way to get some exercise and hang out with their mates. I don't mind. It means I can go out with my friends whenever I want as well, no discussion needed.'

'I'm glad to hear it,' Jaq said, and she was.

She'd worried about how much she would see her best friend from now on.

'So what's up?'

'I landed up sleeping over at Simon's place again.'

Sarah was so astonished she nearly dropped the menu she'd been snatching glances at.

'You and he actually...' Sarah finished the sentence with an explicit hand gesture.

'Nope. I fell asleep at his dining room table. The last time I fell asleep anywhere like that was during our chemistry lessons.'

'I remember that,' Sarah said with a laugh. 'Neither of us could keep our eyes open through those boring things.

But, whatever else I could say about Simon, boring you to sleep isn't it.'

'It wasn't him. I was just so knackered I was out before I knew it.'

'And he left you there? Wait. No. That I can believe.'

'He was also gone by the time I woke up.'

'I see,' Sarah said vaguely, picking up the menu again and giving it a bit more attention, although she'd probably go with her usual, now that she was no longer dieting. 'So... do you like him?'

Jaq shrugged.

'I honestly don't know what's got into me lately. I'm running around like a crazy woman, going on dates every free weekend. But I haven't liked any of the men enough to go beyond dinner or, rarely, a one-night stand.'

'Does that include Rob?'

'I'm letting that fizzle out. I went on a date with him and didn't enjoy it. He was too managing. He decided where we were going, told me what was good on the menu and then looked put out when I didn't choose it. I tried with him, honestly, but I just feel nothing for him.'

'Don't push yourself on my account or do anything just because you're feeling left behind,' Sarah said more seriously.

The waiter turned up at that moment, giving Jaq a chance to gather her thoughts while Sarah ordered an avocado toast for herself and the same for Jaq, who was nodding her agreement.

'I guess it all started when Ellen got married and is now onto her second kid, then all our school and uni friends and now you. Even Noel's talking about marriage.'

'Well, your sister's older than you, so that's understandable.'

'Yeah, but Noel's three years younger than me.'

'But he's been dating the same girl since school.'

'And what about all our other friends? I'm the only remaining singleton.'

'But what do you want from it? You wouldn't be so obsessed if you didn't have a reason.'

'I guess... I want that soulmate everybody else talks about. You know, that person whose shoulder you can cry on when you've had a shitty day. That person who you can be comfortable with, and go on holiday with and go to parties without feeling weird. I want somebody to be close to and somebody who wants to be close to me. God, it all sounds so pathetic when I say it out loud.'

'It isn't all wonderful, you know. Sometimes your so-called soulmate has had his own shitty day, holes up in the garden shed, and has no interest in being your emotional support. Sometimes, being in the same house with someone can be lonelier than actually living alone.'

'God, Sarah, are you alright?' Jaq asked, suddenly worried for her friend.

'It's fine, really. I'd rather be with Aaron than without. It's just the real issues of married couples are spoken about less than the fantasies. Being married takes work.'

'I guess I know that better than most. I did my fair share of breaking up battling spouses when I was a beat cop.'

Jaq didn't mention the family murders she'd seen too. She didn't want to blacken their mood.

Sarah nodded, then waited as the waiter returned and placed their orders before them, leaving salt and pepper grinders in the middle of the table which Jaq dived for. Sarah, as usual, didn't touch them.

'You know,' Sara said as she took a bite out of her toast, 'the one advantage Simon has is that he already knows what you do.'

'All too well.'

Jaq kept to herself her own suspicions about Simon and that his association with the police was not of the best, and that was an understatement.

'He thinks you don't like him.'

'How do you know that?'

'He told me the day after your drunken sleepover. He seemed pretty sure of your opinion. But then again, he isn't that good at understanding people.'

'He also told me to go home. So you're probably right. In that case, I should just leave him alone. After all, I've done what I intended to do: apologise. I have no reason to see him again.'

'And yet, here we are talking about him.'

'Yeah.'

Jaq blinked at Sarah as if she'd pointed out something astonishing.

'Why?' Sarah asked.

'Good question. I suppose... he is good looking.'

'And'

'As you said, he already knows what I do.'

'And?'

'He has a certain... competence,' Jaq said, digging deep because now she was also wondering what drew her to Simon.

'He is good at his job,' Sarah said. 'And you've got to admire what he's achieved, being an orphan and all.'

'Ah... yes.'

Jaq wished she'd asked Simon about his cover story, because she'd just realised she didn't know it and she didn't want to inadvertently expose him. If Sarah knew the truth... Well, she never would. It was best that way.

But really, considering his background, Simon had been amazingly successful. Kids with far less terrible backgrounds had foundered or failed at adult life.

'So what are the cons of a potential relationship with Simon?' Sarah asked.

His criminal past, Jaq thought. But honestly, did it matter if nobody, her colleagues included, would ever know? If they got together, a really unlikely, if, he would merely be her arty-farty, designer boyfriend.

'He doesn't like me.'

'He doesn't date. Although we all recently discovered that he isn't gay,' Sarah said and told Jaq about the intern with a crush. 'You have to hand it to Simon, he'll tell you up front. So you wouldn't have to worry about him being unclear about what he thinks of you.'

'That may be a con if he doesn't like me.'

'At least you won't waste your time chasing after him if he's not interested.'

'Now I just need to work out if I am,' Jaq said, taking a sip of tea.

'We wouldn't be talking about him if you weren't.'

10

— • —

SIMON WAS RELIEVED TO find his home empty and entirely his when he got back laden with his weekly grocery shop. He went to check his cameras as he did each day, running through all the footage. Usually, it was just him leaving for work in the morning and coming back in the evening. Today it showed Jaq wandering around.

At least she'd spotted his note. As with the last time, she'd also taken a shower. He should have put a towel out for her again too, he realised, as she appeared, wrapped in his towel, only long enough to cover what decency required but leaving a lot on view. She was holding her clothes and headed for the washing machine.

An unfamiliar quiver sent a sick sensation through his stomach as he took in the detective's long, muscular legs. Christ, what was that? Sometimes he felt desperate for a bit of intimacy, but it always came with a dollop of nausea.

He felt like a pervert and that he should stop watching, but he didn't. He did put it on fast forward though as he watched the detective emerge from the shower, fetch her clothes and disappear to get dressed. Then she came out again and rummaged through his desk drawers.

What the hell did she think she was doing? She took out his post-it notes and left a message of her own in the fridge.

Simon watched till the end of the recording where she left the house, then hurried to the fridge. Bang in the middle of the tub of curry was a note.

Hi Simon.

You should eat this. Don't let my money go to waste. Also, sorry about falling asleep. It wasn't intentional. Thanks for putting up with me last night and for the blanket.

Jaq xx.

He read it a few times but couldn't wrap his head around what it meant, especially the last bit. His limited experience at work had told him that post-it notes were never signed with a kiss, certainly not two. Not unless the woman was flirting. No matter how he looked at it, Jaq was unlikely to flirt with him.

The decision to put Jaq out of his mind and actually doing it turned out to be two different things. It upset Simon's ability to concentrate on his work and his painting so much that on Monday evening Simon found himself back on Dr Nobel's leather couch.

'I must be quite the basket case, huh?' he said, rubbing his hands together as he gazed at his fingers.

'What makes you say that?' Dr Nobel asked.

It was a familiar opening that made Simon smile despite his embarrassment.

'I just overheard your receptionist telling somebody you don't have an opening for the next six months, but I always get an appointment on the day I call.'

'That's because you're one of my kids.'

'What do you mean?' Simon asked as he looked up into Dr Nobel's reassuring, smiling face.

'There are a handful of you who have a special place in my heart. I am very proud of how you have spread your wings and become a well-functioning member of society.'

'Not so well functioning,' Simon said and went back to staring at his tightly interlocked fingers.

'Do you need a top up of your anti-anxiety meds?'

'No... I've still got half the prescription.'

'That's good to hear. So what do you want to talk about this evening?'

Simon took a deep breath. This was the moment of truth where he had to screw up his courage and speak.

'I... I was wondering whether... whether you thought I could have a... a relationship with a woman?'

Simon was familiar with Dr Nobel's technique of leaving long silences for the patient to fill. It often had him babbling on. But he really had no more, so he looked back up at her. She had her head cocked to the side.

'Do you not have a normal relationship with women? You get on fine with me, and from what you've told me of your colleagues, you get on well with them, too.'

Simon was regretting bringing it up. He'd just realised that Dr Nobel had assumed certain things about him that he was now exposing. It made him feel like he'd failed to live up to her expectations.

'I... I never meet with them alone... women, I mean. I'm too afraid of what might happen.'

'What do you think will happen, Simon?'

'I don't know.' Again the silence that he was expected to fill and this time Dr Nobel looked like she was going to wait. 'I'm afraid of what might happen if I go off with somebody and then they disappear.'

'Why would they disappear?'

'Women disappear all the time. Liz disappeared. All those women Gregory Black went off with disappeared. I know it sounds stupid now that I say it out loud, but it terrifies me,' Simon said, his voice growing tight and his hands beginning to shake.

'Do you fear what you might do if you were alone with them?'

Simon looked up, surprised that Dr Nobel had misunderstood.

'I won't hurt them. I'm just too scared to touch them. And the sounds... when I hear people kissing on the tube, or just... it's the same as when my father... when he was strangling them. Those little gasps and squeaks...'

'I understand,' Dr Nobel said, unexpectedly stepping in. 'This is reaching deep into your trauma and there is no need to go somewhere so painful today.'

Simon sighed with relief and rubbed his hands over his eyes, working on regaining his composure.

'Instead of going over the past. Why don't you tell me what has happened for you to ask your question. Would you like to have a better relationship with women in general, or perhaps there is one woman in particular?'

Of course Dr Nobel would figure it out, Simon thought. Then again, this was why he came to her, to discuss things he couldn't talk to other people about.

'There's this woman... she keeps popping up in my life.'

'I see.'

Damn Dr Nobel and her noncommittal responses.

'I don't think she likes me and I'm pretty sure I don't like her, but I can't stop thinking about her either.'

'When you say, popping into your life, what do you mean?'

'She's one of the detectives who arrested me the other day. But I'd actually met her before at a work do, and after that she and her cop partner asked for my help with some delinquents. Then we fell out over that and she came to apologise, drunk, and landed up sleeping on my carpet. Then she came again to apologise, sober, and fell asleep again. She was still there in the morning, so I went to get groceries, but she was gone by the time I got back. I'd even bought extra food in case she wanted breakfast.'

'And you think this woman dislikes you?' Dr Nobel said and sounded less than her usual neutral self.

'She's a cop, and she knows all about my past, and she's pushy and brusque.'

'So what do you like about her?'

'Like?' Simon said, looking up in surprise. Dr Nobel raised an eyebrow and gave him a nod. But he really had to think about the answer. 'She's pretty, I suppose. Not drop dead gorgeous but... nice. And she's very athletic. Her legs...' Simon blushed. 'She could knock me down without breaking a sweat. But I guess you could say that about most people. I'm a desk bound wimp.'

'What else?'

'She seems really professional and dedicated to her job. When I saw her at the police station, the second time around she was so focussed. No nonsense. I don't know, she seemed really cool.'

'And if you never see her again, what will happen?'

'I guess... I'll just carry on as I was before.'

'And would you want to have a relationship with any other woman?'

Simon tilted his head to consider.

'Sometimes I think so and sometimes a feel like I'm fine the way I am. But... maybe I should try to get over my hangups.'

'You know how I work, Simon,' Dr Noble said as she stepped out from behind her desk and sat down in the club chair next to him.

'Yes, I know, the patient has to want to change, otherwise we can achieve nothing.'

'Would you be okay with taking my hand?' Dr Nobel asked, holding her left hand out, palm up.

'Now?' Simon said, as his stomach constricted with fright.

'You've done Cognitive Behavioural Therapy in the past. You know how it can be helpful.'

'I do,' Simon said, but his hand still shook as he put it on top of Dr Nobel's.

'I just wanted to gauge what we need to do. I won't go further than this today.'

'I'm sorry. I feel like I've let you down,' Simon said, trying not to squirm while holding the doctor's hand.

'No, why?'

'I'm not as well adjusted as you thought.'

'You've just taken a huge step and I'm actually prouder of you now than I've ever been.'

Simon trusted Helen Nobel and usually believed everything she said, but this was a strange reaction to him. He also couldn't concentrate with her holding his hand. He cautiously pulled it away, watching the doctor. She made no comment and simply crossed her hands in her lap.

'So what should I do now?' Simon asked and immediately regretted it because he was supposed to find his own solutions. That was how Dr Nobel worked.

But to his surprise, she said, 'If you are genuinely interested in this woman, then you should try reaching out to her.'

'Really? Me?'

'Dating, especially making that first connection, is difficult for everyone. That whole, do they like me or don't they question is always uppermost in people's minds. From what you've told me, this detective has always been the one to initiate contact. But if you never reciprocate, she'll take that as you not being interested and she'll move on.'

Simon nodded. It made sense. 'But—'

'I'll leave the rest to you. Have a think, and make another appointment with my receptionist if and when you are ready to proceed with the CBT.'

11

'WHY ARE YOU LOOKING so nervous?' Sarah said as she and Simon stood in the gallery's foyer before the massive centrepiece of the company's annual art show. It was an unusual bronze sculpture of a mass of be-suited people wrestling in a towering pile called Modern Babylon. 'Still not convinced that this is the best piece for the entrance hall?'

Simon shrugged. The sculpture was the last thing on his mind.

'It's technically well made, and certainly eye-catching. It will work well in the lobby of some multinational corporation.'

'It would be very ironic if any of them did that,' Sarah said with a laugh. 'The artist specifically states that it's a commentary against mass consumerism and globalisation.'

'Yeah, well, most of the CEOs of massive companies neither know nor care what art symbolises.'

'Not an opinion to be voiced when we've invited as many of those CEOs as we can, along with the great and the good of society.'

'Did you also invite Jaq?'

There was no point in dancing about the question. Sarah would have picked up on his intention even if he tried to be subtle.

'Is that why you've dressed up so nicely?'

It was. Simon had taken special care and was wearing a dark pair of silvery grey trousers and a light grey long sleeved bamboo shirt with a subtle sheen.

'Do you think she'll notice?'

'Jaq notices everything. It goes with the job.'

Simon nodded.

'So you've started liking her, have you?' Sarah said.

'I don't know yet,' Simon said, but he'd never felt more nervous about seeing Jaq before, and that was saying something.

'Boss, other boss, the caterers need you,' Brian said, starting his message when he wasn't quite halfway across the foyer, his voice booming through the space.

'I'll deal with the caterers,' Sarah said. 'I'll leave you and Brian to check on the staff at reception.'

The wink Sarah gave Simon startled him until he realised it was conspiratorial. Was she sending him to reception so that he would be the first to see Jaq arrive?

'No need for you to be at reception, boss,' Brian said. 'Aisha has that fully under control and she might be offended if you butt in.'

'She's quite assertive for an intern,' Simon said as he watched Aisha and the team of company receptionists receiving the first of the guests and handing them their name tags and welcome packs.

'Yeah,' Brian said and started blushing as he added. 'She told me to ask if you'd give us a guided tour of the works later on, you know, once the party is over.'

'She told you to do that, did she?' Simon said, and it actually elicited a smile, despite his nerves. 'Why should I? All the works are described in the catalogue.'

Brian grew redder still as he said, 'They're really excellent descriptions from an artistic perspective. You're good at explaining everything from a design perspective and how we can use artwork and the elements in art for marketing. Aisha says you should teach a course on that at our college.'

Simon laughed but was flattered.

'Okay, come and see me later. Now I'd better mingle.'

Mingling wasn't Simon's favourite occupation. He usually found making small talk laborious, but at least here he had the art he could direct people's attention too. It gave him a topic to work with.

Besides, after seven years with the company, Simon had grown accustomed to these big events. The purpose was to raise the company's profile and drum up business. He'd also got to know many of the people attending as clients and usually started on groups where he knew at least one person before he tried to engage the others.

Simon did fine with the people who actually cared about art. He struggled with those who had merely turned up to see and be seen. He usually moved them along to Sarah and the people from the sales department.

This evening he was less interested in mingling and spent a lot more time scanning people's faces looking for Jaq. Just thinking about approaching her made his hand shake. He see-sawed wildly between planning how he was going to do it and debating whether he should just stay away. Then he'd chide himself for chickening out and start planning all over again.

But Jaq didn't appear. He checked the crowd through their CEO's welcome speech, and again when everyone was clustered about the main hall, helping themselves to the canapes and drinks from the circulating waiters. Simon decided a case must be keeping Jaq away, which left him feeling relieved. No need to screw up his courage tonight, then.

That was when he saw Jaq, dressed in a draped figure hugging silver lamé dress, talking to two men. The first man was unusually tall and towered over her. The other was a sweaty man in his fifties with a ginger moustache and a loud, wheezing laugh that Simon could hear over the chatter. They were both standing so close to Jaq that they had almost backed her against a painting.

She looked unimpressed. This was an ideal moment for him to intervene. Jaq could easily get herself out of the situation, of course, but Simon wanted to help. He put down the glass of champagne he'd been nursing and threaded his way through the crowd.

'Jaq!' Simon said as he approached. 'Here you are. I've been looking everywhere for you so I could show you the Galvani.'

Jaq's momentarily astonished expression morphed into a broad smile. 'Of course, the Galvani. I've been dying to see it.' With that, she nodded a farewell to the men and sailed away with Simon.

'Thank you,' Jaq said. 'You arrived in the nick of time.'

Simon found himself grinning at Jaq, even as he had to shove his right hand in his pocket to hide that it was shaking. He couldn't believe he'd done it!

'You looked fed up. I was afraid of what you might do next.'

'Oh, so you were just protecting your company by stepping in before I caused a scene, were you?' Jaq said with an answering smile. 'Is there even such a thing as a Galvani?'

'Oh yeah. Do you want to see it?'

'We might as well, since I'm supposedly keen on the thing.'

Simon led Jaq into a quieter room where the guests were strolling along the exhibitions, admiring the occasional piece and murmuring their thoughts to their companions. He stopped before a plain white square surrounded by the widest gold frame Jaq had ever seen.

'This is it?' Jaq said, staring at the textured white paper. 'You thought I'd like a plain white square.'

'That isn't the artwork,' Simon said, grinning from ear to ear. He couldn't help himself. He was in his element. This was his home turf, like the police station was Jaq's. 'It's the frame.'

'The frame?' Jaq took a step back to examine the extensive curves and the curling golden carved feathers. 'I don't get it. Sarah always tells me the artist is making a statement on one thing or another, but this one is downright weird. What does it mean?'

'Whatever you want it to mean.'

'Oh, really?' Jaq flipped open her catalogue. 'According to the artist, this piece is a juxtaposition of form over substance, a reflection of how the world interprets art as the thing in the middle without realising art is all around you.'

'Yeah, or he could say some people are all front and no substance. But that doesn't matter. A hundred years from now, if this piece still exists, there will be thousands of interpretations of what it means.'

'Is that a good thing?'

Simon shrugged.

'How does it make you feel when you look at it?'

'Honestly... irritated.' Jaq took a step back so she could see the full glory of the frame. 'My eyes keep being drawn to the plain little square in the middle. If there was a picture, I could cope better. I mean, even when they're selling frames, they put a picture in so you can see how it will look in your house.'

'Yeah, but if you replaced his white square, you'd be accused of destroying the artwork.'

'What nonsense. Honestly, sometimes you artistic types are so weird.'

'I guess so.' Simon wasn't sure where to go next and just blurted out, 'I like your dress,' and instantly regretted it. As a way of making conversation, it sucked.

'Thank you,' Jaq said, and looked flattered. So all was not lost. 'It's by a fashion icon. I wanted something cool for this event. I wore this same dress to your art show last year.'

'You were here last year?' Simon said and wondered why he hadn't noticed her.

'I'm guessing you were too.'

'For the last seven years. Ever since I joined the company.'

'Funny,' Jaq said, shaking her head. 'So, speaking as an artist and a designer, what do you make of the dress?'

It seemed to be a deliberately provocative question, but it gave Simon a chance to take in the glory of Jaq's figure.

'It's beautiful. It suits you.'

'Not too flashy, then?'

'No.' Simon hesitated, uncertain how Jaq would take his next comment. 'But from a design point of view... you might want to change the necklace.'

'Why is that?' Jaq asked, apparently unfazed.

'The dress makes a powerful statement, while the necklace is delicate, with just a small solitaire diamond. It disappears against the dress. A heavier piece of sculptural jewellery in plain silver would complement the dress better.'

'I'll bear that in mind. Or maybe, one day, you can help me pick something more appropriate.'

Simon couldn't work out whether that was a counterattack to his comment or an invitation. He also didn't know which he'd prefer.

12

— · —

ASIDE FROM BEING ABLE to report back to Dr Nobel that he'd approached Jaq and had a half decent conversation before duty dragged him away, Simon still didn't know what he made of Jaq. He also wasn't clear what a next step should or could be, never mind whether he wanted to take it. Fortunately, Jaq was away on holiday, so he knew she wouldn't be turning up unexpectedly.

He realised his feelings were turning more positive towards Jaq when he looked at the date on his phone to work out when Jaq would be back in London. This, of course, didn't mean she'd be in touch.

So Simon shot to his feet when the doorbell rang. Since he wasn't expecting anything, his combined hope and fear was that it was Jaq. The intercom revealed her standing outside, a bag of takeaways held up to the camera like a bribe.

'What is it now?' Simon asked, with only a twinge of anxiety. 'It's nine o'clock.'

'Exactly,' Jaq said with a cheeky grin he assumed was meant to win him over. 'That's why I brought dinner. I hope you like Chinese.'

'Why? Why are you here?' Simon asked, standing his ground for now but torn between letting her in and determination to keep her out. 'It's late.'

'Ah, I'm sorry. The thing is, I'm in the middle of a case and... there's something I'd like to ask you about it.'

'Something you want to ask me?' Simon said and his feeling that he should avoid this woman grew stronger. The last thing he wanted to do was get dragged into thinking about crimes and victims and death.

'Pretty please? It's because of what you told me in the missing boy case.'

'I should have kept my mouth shut.'

'But you didn't, which was what got me to thinking you're one of the good guys,' Jaq said, looking hopeful, but also like she assumed she'd already won the argument.

'Astonishing,' Simon said, and it did amaze him that not only had Jaq appeared, but she wanted to talk about work. He was somewhat glad about the former and not at all happy about the latter. 'Don't you think this is verging on harassment?'

'Oh!' Jaq looked equally surprised. 'If you really don't like it, I'll go. I don't want to make you uncomfortable. It's just, your house is close by and we were told to take a break, so I thought I'd come over. I'm really sorry.'

Simon blinked at her, trying to process her change in attitude. Was she really as crestfallen as she appeared or was this just some world class interrogator style manipulation?

'No, it's okay,' he said, with mixed feelings about encouraging her. Then again, he'd made the first move at the gallery and he had to work out what he really wanted. 'But I don't want to know anything about the case you're working on.'

'Deal!' Jaq had already turned to leave, but at his words, she swung back and sailed into the house. 'Come on, let's eat. I assume you haven't eaten yet.'

Aside from a bit of dried fruit, he hadn't. When he was home alone, he couldn't work up much enthusiasm for food.

'I got a couple of side dishes with vegetables. I suspect you don't eat enough greens,' Jaq said as she opened a series of take away tubs. 'Oh nice, their stir-fried broccoli is bright green. I was worried it might be overcooked, but it's perfect.'

Simon peered at the food as he handed a plate and cup to Jaq and then laid another for himself. He'd brought cutlery as well, but Jaq was already snapping apart a pair of chopsticks. So he sat down and tried to decide between egg fried rice or the stir-fried noodles.

He couldn't stop himself from continuously glancing at Jaq. No matter how he looked at it, this was all bloody weird.

'You're not used to this, are you?' Jaq said.

'What?'

Even the question, innocuous as it was, pushed up his anxiety.

'Eating with just one other person. Sarah told me you never do it. Why is that?'

'Are you interrogating me now?'

'Sorry, I was just curious. But if you don't want to answer, don't worry.'

Jaq spoke without looking up as she slurped up part of a slice of something white that she'd mentioned was turnip. The other vegetable dish.

Not having her penetrating gaze on him gave Simon the courage to say, 'I'm trying to keep myself safe.'

'Safe from what?'

'From whatever might happen if that person disappeared.' It sounded stupid saying it out loud. 'Not that it helped in the end.'

'That sounds a bit paranoid, if you don't mind me saying so.'

Interrogation 101, Simon assumed, because Jaq was still not making eye contact, focusing instead on her dinner. It made it easier to talk, but not easy. Should he just tell her to stop?

'I was brought up to be paranoid.'

Christ, he'd said it. Something he thought he'd never speak of again was out in the open with this woman who knew... really knew about him. No need to pretend to have had a normal childhood with her.

'He told me I'd go to jail for what I was doing and what I was seeing. He said if I ever let anyone suspect, he'd kill me.'

'Do you never call him your dad?' Jaq said, her voice level verging on disinterested.

'He was no father. I disowned him. I try to never think about him.'

Simon's hand was shaking. It was impossible to eat, so he put the chopsticks down on the side of his plate and focused on breathing and getting himself under control.

'I'm sorry,' Jaq said, and this time she did look up and gave him a sympathetic smile. 'People always feel sorry for victims of crime and their families, but there's precious little sympathy for the families of perpetrators. Sometimes with good reason, but often they are victims too.

'They suffer a double shock. First because of what their relative did, and second, the revulsion and ostracism from those around them. So I can understand why you live the way you live. But if it helps, you have a friend in me, and I'm not just saying that because you have helped me out.'

'Thank you... I guess.'

It was strange to hear a member of the police force call him a friend. It didn't feel right — too soon. Then again, he wasn't accustomed to making friends, so he had no idea when you could start calling a person a friend. Simon wondered whether it would be possible to push her away, even if he wanted to. It seemed unlikely.

'No really,' Jaq said with a smile. 'After all, we've met three times socially and this is our second time over takeaways. I'd say we're getting on well. Test me, ask a friend related question.'

Simon had no idea what that was supposed to be and thought her assessment was far too optimistic. Still, there was something he was curious about.

'I've been wondering about your name. Is it like Jack the Ripper?'

'Like Jaqueline, except I never liked that name, too girly. Have some broccoli. I promise it won't kill you.'

Simon obediently put a couple of florets of broccoli on his plate and mixed them into his rice. Whether he'd eat them was still to be determined. Then he glanced back at Jaq, absorbed in her food again. Or just good at looking that way.

What was it she'd said, though? Oh yeah, she ate when she was stressed. She must be really stressed, judging by the way she was tucking in. He didn't want to know the reason and instead manfully crunched into one of the pieces of broccoli. It was not his favourite vegetable, but this one wasn't too bad since the garlic, ginger and sesame oil they had fried it in obscured its flavour.

'How was your holiday?'

'Just what I needed. A caravan practically on the beach, lots of walks, lots of sunbathing. The weather was perfect for a change, and long chats over a glass of wine with Ellen.'

'Your sister?'

'Yep. Her husband stayed home to look after my nephew, and it was nice to have her to myself. Otherwise, her attention is always divided.'

'Mmm,' Simon said and stuffed another piece of broccoli into his mouth to prevent having to say more on a subject he had no knowledge about.

'You'd have liked the skies. It became our tradition to sit on the porch of the caravan with a glass of wine and watch the sun gently sink beneath the sea. The way the clouds lit up was spectacular. The sea looked amazing too. I think you'd have liked to paint it,' Jaq said, waving her chopsticks to encompass his cloud paintings. 'Unless you only do clouds.'

'Do you think just painting clouds is boring?'

'I meant no offence.'

'I've never seen the sea,' Simon said, and it took some effort to confess this.

He expected Jaq's reaction. It was the same reason he'd stopped saying things like this to his colleagues.

'Seriously, you've never been to the sea? You, who lives only an hour's train ride away from the sea in two directions, have never seen it.'

Simon nodded. 'I'd want to see it before I tried to paint it.'

'But, I mean, you could use photos or even video. I mean, you know what the sea looks like, don't you?'

'Of course. But unless I experience it for myself, it would feel fake trying to paint it.'

'Fake? I don't get it.'

'It's okay. I don't expect you to understand.'

'Why? Because I'm just a thick copper?'

Simon was taken aback.

'Because you're not a painter, that's all.'

'Ah, sorry, I shouldn't have snapped. I'm tired and it's making me grumpy.'

Simon nodded and, for a change, kept his eyes on Jaq. He hardly knew her, which didn't match what he knew about friends. How did one get to know somebody? He was pretty sure he'd never tried to do that before with anyone.

'You can explain cloud paintings to me another time. I have a feeling it's too technical for my tired brain to cope with today,' Jaq said with an apologetic smile. 'What else can we talk about? Books. I notice you don't have any in this very elegant flat of yours.'

Simon threw back his head with a sigh and gazed at the roof, wondering whether he should just ask Jaq to leave. She was stressful at the best of times, but a tired and pushy Jaq was harder, especially when he had to figure out where she was going with her questions.

'I'm not very good at reading. When I got to the young offenders' institution, they did some tests and discovered I have dyslexia.'

'Really? That thing where you can't read and write very well?'

'Yeah. Reading is a struggle. It's very tiring, so I mostly get my information from videos and I watch films and box sets for my entertainment.'

'But your handwriting is so beautiful. How is that possible?'

'I get around writing by thinking of it as drawing. What you saw wasn't actually my handwriting, just my drawing of Kushan Script. It's one of my favourite fonts. If I draw that, it's neat. If I try to write in my own style, it's a mess.'

'Wow, that's amazing. So they didn't sort out your reading and writing at school?'

'I didn't go to school.'

Jaq's surprised expression turned to one of deep thought, and then she nodded.

'I'm sorry, again. In fairness, you can ask me absolutely any question you like about me.'

'Why do you keep coming here?'

Simon feared it was too rude, and too sudden, but it was the only thing he truly wanted to know.

'Oh,' Jaq said with a half sigh, half laugh as she put the chopsticks down and gave him the first embarrassed look Simon had seen from her. 'I'm not sure I've worked that out for myself yet, either.'

'Ah,' Simon said and, since he couldn't think of a followup question, he picked another piece of broccoli out of the container and put it in his mouth.

The sound of him crunching his way through it was painfully loud in the silent room. He didn't dare look up to see what Jaq was thinking but watched her chopsticks hover over the tubs laid out on the table, picking a mouthful of noodles and then a blob of turnip slice.

'What about Rob?' Simon asked, surprising himself that he was curious about Jaq's relationship with the man.

'What about him?' Jaq said with a mysterious smile. 'Do you not go after women who are already taken?'

Simon gasped and sat back, cursing his unruly mouth. 'That's not...'

How could he say it wasn't what he meant, or that he'd never coveted any woman before, taken or otherwise?

'What do you think of Rob?' Jaq asked, back to picking at her food.

'He's a good salesman.'

'So he keeps telling me, but that's a very neutral comment. Does that mean you don't like him?'

Simon shrugged. He hadn't considered the question before.

'He's a bit... boastful.'

'Irritatingly so. And just in case you've got the wrong idea, there is nothing going on between me and Rob.'

Maybe Jaq was telling the truth about that, but Simon wondered whether Rob would agree and also why Jaq was telling him that. He realised she'd laid her chopsticks down across her plate and was yawning prodigiously. She hastily covered her hand with her mouth, blinking back the tears of sleep.

'Sorry about that. It's been a long, hard week.'

'How long of a break were you going to take?'

Jaq shrugged. 'Three, four hours. Just not long enough to be able to go home.'

'Why not?'

'I live too far away. It's an hour long commute, the joys of living in London. I bought my place when it was still affordable and I worked locally. Then I got transferred and I can't afford to sell and move, so I'm stuck with the commute.'

Simon nodded. At least his commute to work was only half an hour. That made him the envy of most of the people in the office.

'And you said you wanted to ask me something,' Simon said because, despite trying not to think about it, he was curious.

'Ah yes. The thing is, my current case, without going into detail, is about school violence. The team has the feeling there's more to it than kids breaking into gangs. There's a level of sophistication that's surprising even for older high schoolers. So I was wondering if you think there might be someone behind it. Like with Chazza.'

'Are they linked in some way?' Simon asked, although with the level of information he'd been given, it was the vaguest of guesses.

'Same neighbourhood.'

Simon shook his head, trying to think how best to explain.

He took a deep breath and said, 'Gregory Black used a mixture of indoctrination, coaxing and threats to make me to follow his lead. He had such control, I could hardly think for myself. What I saw with Chazza, just for an instant, was that same look of confusion. As if he couldn't pin down where things were going wrong. If the whole thing had been his plan, he wouldn't have looked as lost.'

'So you think an adult is behind this? Somebody close to these kids?'

'How would I know? With the internet they could control them from anywhere.'

'Mmm, not to this degree. I have a feeling you'd need much closer contact to control what's going on here,' Jaq said and yawned so widely her eyes squeezed shut. 'God, I'm tired.'

'Can't you take a nap?'

'Ha, my options are under my desk or the men's changing room, because the ladies' is currently being renovated and is covered in plaster dust.'

'Oh,' Simon said, and his pulse quickened at the immediate solution that occurred. The offer hovered on the tip of his tongue, wrestling with ongoing indecision. 'You can nap on my sofa if you like.'

Jaq paused mid stretch and blinked at him.

'Really?'

'It wouldn't be the first time.'

'Yeah,' Jaq said and had the grace to look embarrassed. 'I'm sorry about that.'

Simon shrugged and went to fetch the fleece he'd given her before from the entrance hall cupboard.

'Thanks,' Jaq said, giving him a brilliant smile as she took it. 'I hope you're not offended if I go to sleep now?'

'No, of course...' Simon said, gave her an uncertain nod and watched as she first set up an alarm on her phone, then wrapped herself in the fleece and rolled over so that she was facing the back of the sofa.

Simon gathered up the uneaten food and the dirty plates and, working as quietly as possible, washed the dishes. Then he tiptoed to his room, glancing at a lightly snoring Jaq, and killed some time watching videos in bed. A couple of hours later, he heard the creak of his front door, and then a clunk as it shut again. Jaq had left, and Simon could finally fall asleep.

In the morning Simon found a bright yellow post it on the fridge door.

Thanks for letting me kip at yours. I can't tell you how grateful I was.

Finish the damn leftovers, you skinny man.

Jaq xx

13

'ARGH, BLOODY MONITORING PAPERWORK,' Jaq muttered for the hundredth time as she scowled at her computer screen.

'How far have you got?' Darren asked, not looking up from his own pile, actual papers in his case, labels for all the evidence they'd gathered.

'I am at form 36 of 52.'

'At least you're past halfway.'

Darren sounded relaxed. Maybe it was because he was older that he seemed to enjoy the downtime they had between cases.

'I swear we spend more time reporting on our casework than actually solving crimes.'

Jaq didn't expect a reply. She always said the same things when they wrapped up a case, and she already knew what Darren's response would be.

She'd just pressed save on form 36 and started pondering whether she should have lunch before she tackled the next form when her office phone rang.

'Excuse me, ma'am,' the desk sergeant said as she picked up. 'I have a call for you from somebody called Simon White. He said it has something to do with Sarah. He said you'd know what he means.'

At the sound of Sarah's name, Jaq's stomach gave a frightened twist and she snapped, 'Put him through.'

'Ah... Jaq?' Simon said, his voice sounded odd and tinny on the phone. 'Sorry to bother you—'

'Get to the point,' Jaq snapped. 'What's happened to Sarah?'

'She's ill. I've taken her to A&E, the thing is, Aaron is in Edinburgh on business and HR doesn't have any other family contacts for her.'

'Which hospital?' Jaq said, and she noted Darren's head snap up as he gave her a querying look. She got the hospital name from Simon and said, 'I'll be there in half an hour,' as she slammed the phone down.

'Work?' Darren said.

'Personal. I'm sorry I have to go.'

Darren waved her off and Jaq ran all the way to the tube station. It would be quicker than trying to get through London's congested streets by car.

Public transport being what it was, it took her forty-five minutes to get to the hospital. It took another frustrating thirty minutes to convince reception to give her Sarah's location until she resorted to flashing her badge. This elicited the information that they had moved Sarah from A&E into a ward.

The fact that it had happened so quickly alarmed Jaq and made her worry all the more about Sarah. People usually spent hours in A&E. Despite her anxiety, she walked all the way, following the blue line marked on the floor.

Simon's familiar figure, standing in the middle of the corridor speaking to a fresh faced youngster, provided her final clue for tracking Sarah down.

'You may as well go back to the office,' he was saying to the kid.

'Simon!' she said, keeping her voice low for the sake of the patients she could see via the glass windows in each ward door.

He swung round and a look of relief suffused his face.

'She's in there,' he said, pointing at the door to his left. 'They won't let me in because I'm not family.'

'I'll deal with it.' No hospital rule would keep Jaq out. 'Do you know what's wrong?'

Simon shook his head.

'Maybe food poisoning. She was throwing up all morning and then she collapsed.'

'Poor thing,' Jaq said and pushed her way into Sarah's ward.

It was the usual spartan, six-bed ward. All the beds were occupied and it took a moment to find Sarah in the one by the window. She looked frighteningly pale.

'Sarah,' Jaq said softly as she stopped by her side.

'Jaq,' Sarah said with a relieved smile. 'I guess Simon called you. I told him not to bother.'

'Fortunately, he didn't listen. I also called Aaron. He's arranging a flight back.'

'Honestly, there's no need for all this fuss,' Sarah said, but alarmed Jaq with her listlessness.

'They hauled you into A&E, love, and they gave you a bed. They don't do that unless it's serious. Have they worked out what's wrong yet?'

Sarah shook her head.

'They've taken about a pint of blood for tests, though.'

'How long have you been feeling ill? You should have called me.'

'I didn't want to bother everybody. It's been three or four days, but this morning was the worst. I was actually about to head off to the doctors. I'd packed up my bag and everything when I collapsed in the office. It was so embarrassing.'

'Don't stress about it. I'll bet they're all just worried for you.'

'Thank God for Simon, though. Everybody else went into a flap. He just swooped in, calm as you please, helped me to my feet, ordered Brian to take my other side and got Aisha to hail a cab.'

'That was good thinking, a cab is always faster than an ambulance.'

'That's what he said when everybody else objected. And he made sure the nurses in A&E took me in right away. I didn't realise what a good guy he was to have in an emergency till today.'

Jaq wished she could hear more, but was prevented by the appearance of a doctor, trailed by a couple of other white-coated individuals.

'Sarah Parker?' the doctor said as she looked up from the glowing screen of her tablet.

'Yet, that's me.' The doctor looked Jaq up and down with a questioning expression and Sarah said, 'She's my best friend.'

'I'm about to discuss confidential medical information. Are you sure you want your friend to stay?'

'I do,' Sarah said and reached out to take Jaq's hand.

She wasn't the clingy type, so Jaq realised she was feeling less than her usual confident self. With good reason, the doctor looked serious.

'What's the matter with me?'

'You have a severe case of morning sickness,' the doctor said, her expression softening.

'Excuse me, what?' Sarah said.

Jaq was more shocked, maybe because she'd been expecting a different diagnosis.

'You're pregnant. I assume you didn't know that yet?'

'I'm pregnant?'

'Congratulations. Although I'm afraid you're suffering from an extreme form of morning sickness, which means you're going to have to stay in the hospital so that we can ensure you receive sufficient fluids and nutrition. This is an entirely manageable situation in this day and age, but would have been fatal in previous eras. I have booked a specialist to come and give you all the information you need. In the meantime, all you have to do is rest and give your body a chance to recuperate.'

'Oh my God,' Sarah murmured as she watched the doctor and her entourage leaving the ward.

'Congratulations,' Jaq said. 'So you had no idea?'

'None. I mean, Aaron and I have discussed having children. We'd like to someday... I guess this is just sooner than we'd planned.'

'I'm just glad it's nothing more serious.'

While Jaq was happy for Sarah, she could also feel her own envy along with a sense of being left behind.

'Don't tell anyone yet, please, not till I've spoken to Aaron.'

'Don't worry, my lips are sealed. Now I'd best be going. My paperwork, sadly, doesn't finish itself.'

'I'm really grateful that you came.'

'As if I wouldn't.' Jaq's laugh sounded a bit strained, hopefully only to her. 'Get some sleep. Like the doctor said, you need to rest and by the time you wake up, Aaron will be here.'

Simon stood in the middle of the hospital corridor wondering what he should do. He'd delivered Sarah to the hospital, sent Brian back and called Jaq. Now... did he stay to confirm that Sarah was alright, or did he just go back to work?

He was more shaken than he'd allowed himself to show. Simon supposed that after seven years of working with her, he'd developed more respect, or was that friendly affection, for Sarah than he'd realised. He really hoped she would be alright, especially when he saw the large group of doctors that headed into her ward.

He peered through the door and saw them cluster around Sarah, Jaq hovering beside her like a fierce police dog. So now he knew what to do. He'd wait to find out how Sarah was, then head back to work. It presumably wouldn't take very long.

In the meantime, he might as well sit, since there was a row of chairs bolted to the wall opposite. It didn't take long for the doctors to reappear, and a little after that Jaq emerged, looking sombre.

'Is she alright?' Simon asked, leaping to his feet.

'She'll be fine.'

Jaq's behaviour was odd. She seemed both relaxed and upset.

'Are you sure she's okay?'

'There's nothing life threatening, although she will be in the hospital for a few more weeks. I can't tell you more. I'm sorry.'

'No, that's okay,' Simon said, turning to leave. 'As long as she's going to be better soon.'

'Wait,' Jaq said, and her police training made it sound like an order. It stopped Simon and he turned back to her. 'I'm starving. I was just about to have lunch when you called. Do you fancy joining me for a quick bite?'

Simon didn't feel like eating. He seldom did after emotional upheaval. But he also didn't feel like having his arm twisted by Jaq and she wouldn't let him just slip away.

'I don't think the hospital has much in the way of places to eat. There's a coffee shop, though.'

'Ug no, I'm not eating in a hospital. I've done that far too often. There's a cafe outside on the High Street. Why don't we go there?'

'There's a cafe?'

'Didn't you notice it?'

'I was kind of distracted.'

'It's called Rosie's. It's right next to a barber and opposite a hardware store.'

'You noticed all of that?'

'And the makes, colours and licence plates of the cars parked outside at 2:16 as I was walking in.'

'Wow,' Simon said and followed Jaq out.

A cafe would be better than anything they'd find in the hospital, and cheaper. As was his habit, Simon scanned for CCTV as they walked down the High Street and was reassured to see one pointed in the cafe's direction. The eatery itself had a green and white striped awning, only half extended, and the name of the establishment, along with a subscript: *better than hospital food*.

'They aren't exactly selling it, are they?' he murmured.

'What would you do to improve things?' Jaq said with a laugh.

'I'd add a word. Miles... miles better than hospital food. That would work.'

'Yeah, you're right,' Jaq said and strode confidently into the cafe, looking neither right nor left.

Simon was certain she was taking in way more than him, though. In answer to her enquiring look, Simon selected the table by the window where, apart from reflections, they were most likely to be captured by the camera.

Jaq sat with her back to it and said, 'Really, even here you made sure you're surveilled? Why this obsession to be filmed?'

Simon had never been asked this question before, and he wasn't sure how to answer it.

'Same as with my house, the CCTV keeps me safe.'

'How? How on earth does it keep you safe? Believe me, as a detective, they're really useful, but only for figuring out what happened after somebody is attacked or murdered. It doesn't prevent crime.'

'No, but if something happens... if somebody goes missing, I will have proof that it wasn't me.'

Jaq blinked at him, clearly flummoxed by his interpretation.

'But you don't have to worry today. I mean, you're out with a cop.'

'Yeah, but what if something happened to you? With my record, I'd have the entire Met come down on me like a ton of bricks.'

Jaq laughed.

'Don't worry, nothing's going to happen to me.'

Simon wished he could feel as confident and blushed to have his anxieties exposed. To prevent having to say more, he looked over to the counter on the far end and examined the chalkboard listing the dishes of the day.

'What can I get for you, loves?' A middle-aged plump bottle blonde said as she strolled over, pen and paper in hand.

'I'll have your all day breakfast please,' Jaq said with enthusiasm.

'Tea or coffee?'

'Coffee, and orange juice.'

'Toast or fresh?'

'Toast.'

'Crusty or...'

Simon's mind wandered as the waitress went through her interminable list and he had to be called back to attention to give his order.

'Ham and cheese toastie,' Simon said, for want of any other options.

'With or without salad, love?' the woman asked.

'Without,' Simon said, then wondered whether Jaq might make a comment about him not eating vegetables. Fortunately, the waitress didn't give time for that as she asked, 'and to drink? Tea, coffee, soda?'

'Tea,' Simon said, and the waitress nodded, then ambled away to deliver their order.

Since it was the middle of the afternoon, the cook didn't have anyone else and was gazing out at them through his little hatch.

'Mmm, this is nice,' Jaq said as she leaned back in her chair, stretching her arms above her head. 'There's something very homely about a cafe, don't you think?'

Simon looked over the pale green formica-topped tables, Lino floor and tourist posters of Crete on the walls and said, 'I suppose they are all quite similar in appearance.'

'I guess I just like them from childhood. My family would often land up at a cafe after the Saturday morning shop. Mum said she couldn't face making lunches for everyone after she'd spent a hellish morning shepherding us through the supermarket. How about you? Do you like cafes too?'

Simon examined Jaq's face, trying to work out whether she was digging for information or had just asked as a throw away conversation piece.

'Um... the first time I went to a cafe was when I was 18,' he said, aware this would remind her of his past, which he didn't want.

Her suddenly more alert expression showed that she'd realised this too.

'Sorry, I didn't mean to pry.'

Her apology surprised him, and he shrugged. 'Dr Nobel took me on an outing so I could get used...' he paused, looked around and lowered his voice. 'So I could get used to living outside.'

'Was she your therapist?'

Simon nodded.

'Eighteen, huh? I don't even remember the first time I went to a cafe. What did you think?'

'I don't really remember. I was a bit nervous.'

'I guess that's understandable. Do you remember what you had?'

'Cherry pie and custard,' Simon said, surprised that he remembered that.

'You and Doctor Nobel?'

'And Peter the Cheetah.'

'Who?' Jaq said with a surprised laugh.

Simon checked again that the waitress wasn't listening, and said, 'He was one of the guards. He usually went along when the guys were given their first day pass from the young offenders' institution to make sure nobody ran off. Peter was faster than all of them.'

'I have a feeling he didn't have to chase you.'

Simon assumed that was because Jaq thought he was a weak-willed wimp.

'I was so scared I was shaking from head to foot. Peter spent most of the time keeping me upright.'

There, now she had the truth and, if anything was needed to make a strong woman like Jaq back away, it would be that. Her face showed no disgust though, and her neutral expression turned to one of delight as their food arrived. Jaq's breakfast turned out to be doubles of everything, the eggs, sausages, bacon, toast, mushrooms and beans. The sight of all of that food alarmed Simon.

'Are you sure Sarah is alright?'

'What?' Jaq said, thrown by the question.

'You said you were a stress eater and that,' Simon said, waving at the overflowing plate, 'is a lot of food.'

'She's fine, I promise.'

'That's good. I really don't want to take over her role.'

'Why not? Don't you want a promotion?'

'Do you?' Simon said, although the question was unnecessary.

He was pretty sure Jaq was ambitious.

'Of course I do. But not all the way to the top. I want to do the work I trained for, solving crimes. I don't want to go into management.'

'Same here. If you move into management, you do less design work and more people management, and that isn't what I care about.'

'There you go,' Jaq said as she sliced into a juicy sausage, 'we have something in common.'

That pulled Simon up short. Had Jaq been looking for things that made them compatible? He doubted they'd have much in common.

'I hope I didn't call you away from anything urgent.'

'Not at all,' Jaq said, swirling a piece of toast in an egg yolk. 'In fact, you rescued me from the tedium of paperwork, which I was happy to leave to my partner.'

'So you solved that case... with the school?'

'Not entirely to my satisfaction. I can't tell you much, but let's just say no mastermind was found, although even Darren now thinks it's a possibility that there is one.'

'Who?'

'Darren, my partner.'

'Oh... well, I hope you find him, if he does exist.'

'You think he's a man?'

'Wouldn't he be?'

'I don't know,' Jaq said, skewering a slice of bacon and wobbled it about in Simon's direction. 'It's best not to jump to conclusions and to remember that women can be master manipulators as well.'

14

J AQ'S CONVERSATION WITH SIMON had piqued her
curiosity and she mulled over what she knew, dodging
sightseers, as she walked along the Thames heading for the
restaurant Rob had booked. She'd been so worried about
the fact that Simon had a record that she hadn't really
thought about his life before and during that time. All
she'd known was his father had used Simon as bait to lure
women in.

She'd also worked out that the father had made his son
paranoid enough to ensure he had witnesses to everything
he did, albeit the glassy eye of surveillance cameras. Now
the new information that the first time he'd been to a
cafe was when his therapist took him to one at the age of
eighteen. So what had his father been doing with his son
in the meantime?

So many questions and she had access to his record
and the court proceedings so she could learn all about it.
Despite this, she kept putting off taking a look. It was a
typical push pull effect. She was wildly curious as a cop,
and as a person but also scared about what she'd find out
and how that might change their relationship.

Although relationship was straining the definition.
They knew each other. They had interacted on a couple

of occasions. She'd even slept over, something she didn't even do with a one-night stand. Yet, she kept her emotional distance, unwilling to get too close.

She could say the same for Simon. More so. He made no moves to encourage her at all. He'd probably be glad if he never saw her again.

Or would he? She'd have been certain if he hadn't approached her at the art gallery and rescued her from the tedium.

She'd gone intending to scope out the talent. Sarah had promised a multitude of wealthy CEOs. It turned out they were either married or arrogant bores or both. And all the while, she'd been dodging Rob. Fortunately, he'd been too busy schmoozing VIPs to notice her.

But now she had to see him for one last time. He'd invited her to dinner in his usually non consultive way of sending her a date, time and venue and asking if she wanted to join him. So she would, but this would be the end.

As expected, the restaurant was in one of the swanky new developments along the Thames, with a fabulous view of St Pauls. Rob was already there, having a lager at the bar.

'Jaq,' he said, grinning widely as he came over and gave her a hug and a kiss, 'it's great to see you again.'

This type of greeting wasn't her favourite, but it seemed to be Rob's standard, as he's also given Sarah a hug and kiss when they'd all gone out together.

'How are you?' Jaq asked, stepping back out of reach.

'Great, great, you're looking well, at least, you look like you've got more sleep lately.'

'That I have,' Jaq said, hoping Rob didn't ask why she'd been working so hard it impacted her sleep.

'Shall we eat?' Rob asked as the maitre'd had appeared looking relaxed but ready.

'We may as well,' Jaq said, taking in the high ceilings, modern smoky glass chandeliers and full-length windows with the superb London view. This was going to be a very expensive meal.

'I'm more than happy to treat you,' Rob murmured as they threaded their way between the tables.

'There's no need,' Jaq said, and waited for the waiter to pull out her chair for her.

Rob settled opposite and said, 'What is it that you do exactly? You've never told me. You're clearly very busy with whatever it is.'

Jaq had been expecting the question. People in London rarely went straight for the what do you do question. But after a couple of dates, it would be weird not to mention what she did.

Since she was about to draw a line with Rob, she didn't want to tell him now, because he'd tell everyone he worked with, too. She picked up the menu and looked over the opulent offerings, with the expected matching prices. Rob waited for a second, then also picked up the menu with a resigned shrug.

Jaq decided on the steak with red wine jus, creamy celeriac mash and summer beans, which she relayed to the waiter. Rob ordered the lobster, which Jaq felt was just him showing off, and an expensive bottle of red wine. The colour may have been for her benefit, but she doubted it.

Jaq handed the menu to the waiter and said nothing until he'd left before she turned back to Rob.

'Would you keep it a secret if I told you what I did?'

Rob looked up from the menu in astonishment.

'Why? Are you a spy or something? Would you have to kill me if I told anybody?'

'It's nothing that dramatic,' Jaq said, shaking her head. A spy would probably get a more positive response. 'I'm in the police force.'

Rob blinked at her, and she could see the cogs turning. People had weird ideas about the police. Some were fans, others were immediately negative. It always imposed a strain on the conversation.

'So...' Rob said, still digesting the information, 'when you say you're in the police force, what does that mean exactly? Are you a uniformed officer, keeping our streets safe?'

He made it sound jokey, but there was a familiar edge of nerves to it. He was probably doing a mental check of unpaid fines and other possible misdemeanours.

'I'm a Detective Inspector,' Jaq said with a straight face to make sure he got the gravity of her job and that she wasn't joking around. 'Serious Crimes.'

'Wow,' Rob said. 'Okay, I surrender. You can put the cuffs on me.'

It was an all too familiar response. Some men immediately went for the handcuffs, bondage thing. Rob looked undecided.

'This is why I don't tell people.'

'But you have to eventually, right?'

'I suppose so, but I'd appreciate if you don't spread the news around the office. There are security reason as well for keeping quiet about my job.'

'My lips are sealed,' Rob said. 'I assume Sarah knows what you do.'

'Yeah, she does. She knew from before I even went to police college that this was the career I wanted to pursue.'

Rob nodded and leaned back for the waiter to put the food down in front of him. The size of the lobster, and the beautiful way it had been arrayed on a bed of salad greens, impressed Jaq. Her steak arrived, already sliced and the small portion size she'd expected.

'Does Simon know?' Rob asked.

'Know what?' Jaq asked, momentarily thrown.

'That you're a detective.'

Jaq contemplated lying for only a second.

'He knows.'

'So you told him before you told me, but we both met you on that same day at the pub, didn't we?'

'It just worked out that way,' Jaq said as she sliced one of her slivers of beef in half, dipped it in the thin gravy and popped it into her mouth.

It was delicious and she was determined to enjoy it despite the trickiness of the conversation. She supposed being a detective had hardened her to this kind of confrontation.

'And you hung out with him at the art show, too.'

So she had been spotted. That was a shame.

'He rescued me from a particularly obnoxious pair of corporates.'

Jaq wondered whether she'd have gone looking for Simon if he hadn't appeared before her. She was undecided.

'And then? Have you been trying to date him too?'

'This isn't about Simon. This is about what I think of you and what I think our relationship is. And I have to say,

I think it's run its course. I've had fun, but I can't see it turning into anything deeper.'

Rob paused halfway through cracking open a lobster's claw and stared at her.

'Are you dumping me?'

'Honestly, Rob, I don't even think we've been properly dating up till now.'

'Is that your analytical detective's opinion?'

'It's just how I feel. You're a fun guy to go out with, but it's no more than that for me. I'm sorry.'

'You won't get anywhere with Simon, you know? I've stopped counting the number of women who've had a go at him and failed. That whole unobtainable guy thing seems to act like a magnet for women.'

'That's vaguely insulting,' Jaq said, as she took a sip of wine. 'But if you must know, I'm not chasing after him, either. I went to the art show to meet men and just happened to run into Simon.'

'So you're aiming for somebody who earns even more, is that it?'

'More money wouldn't hurt, but that's not my main driver.'

'What is?'

'Somebody compatible, somebody I really, really like.'

'And that's not me?'

'Not at the moment.'

'Huh!' Rob said and speared a piece of lobster quite savagely. 'That's a shame. I thought we had some chemistry.'

Jaq nodded. Rob was so self-confident he probably assumed everyone loved him.

Jaq never enjoyed breaking up with people, be it ever so civilised. At least Rob had got over his disappointment pretty quickly and they'd finished the meal on reasonable terms. Jaq had agreed this would be for the best, as they'd probably continue to see each other through Sarah and Aaron.

Now Jaq was curled up on her little sofa, in her tiny flat, gazing at the chintzy rose wall paper that she'd been meaning to paint over for the last decade, a soothing glass of wine in one hand, her laptop balanced on her knees.

Rob's comments about chasing the unobtainable had really irritated her. She wasn't chasing Simon, although she wasn't so sure that he was impossible to snag. Difficult, certainly, but she had one advantage. She knew about his past. It was the kind of past people kept buried but would probably always nag at the back of his mind as something he was keeping from others.

Just being the son of a notorious serial killer was bad enough. Being a part of his crimes was even worse. So now Jaq simply had to know exactly what part Simon played in everything. That would help her decide whether she stopped what was ultimately not a great career move, or carried on.

She'd remained friends with some men she'd dated. She might become friends with Simon. He seemed not to have any friends at all and might resist, but if she worked carefully and respected his boundaries, maybe they could at least have that.

Jaq took a deep sip of wine to fortify herself and typed her password into the police database. A twinge of guilt made her hesitate before she called up Simon's files. Then she decided that he'd never tell her everything, because the telling would probably be too painful. So she pressed return and a whole host of documents unpacked itself from the file marked Adrian Black aka Simon White.

The first thing Jaq looked at was the arrest record. It was there she discovered that Simon had been fourteen when he'd been discovered. Which was the most appropriate word for breaking through his locked bedroom door. It turned out Simon's birth had never been recorded and prior to going in the police had no idea he was even in the house.

Subsequent investigation had never discovered the name or whereabouts of his mother. She may have been a victim of Gregory Black's, or simply a short-lived relationship. There was no record of a marriage either, and Black had taken the secret of who the woman was to his grave. Simon, according to the records, had no memory of any women living in the house, let alone his mother.

DNA tests had confirmed that Simon was indeed Black's son. Jaq wondered how that must have felt. A part of Simon surely hoped that he shared nothing with such a monster.

Jaq flicked through photos of Simon's bedroom. The furniture was plain and had the look of something that was bought in the seventies and never updated. The carpet was a dirty orange. A simple wooden single bed jutted out into the middle of the room. Aside from that was a wardrobe, a child sized desk piled high with scattered papers and a matching wooden chair. The small bedroom window was barred and looked across the narrow side passage of the house onto the neighbour's garden fence.

So far, so ordinary, if old-fashioned. But what Jaq had temporarily blocked out were the walls. They were covered to about two-thirds of the way up with black scrawls that made the room oppressive.

Jaq flicked through the picture files to all the closeups of the wall. There were thousands. Many were just staring eyes and gaping mouths, black blobs of scratching out so deep it had scraped through the wallpaper and the plasterboard beneath. As she got to the images higher up the wall, there was more detail, presumably because Simon was older, and his drawing technique had improved. Here were grotesque images of women being strangled, tongues lolling out, eyes starting, arms flung wide, a man leering over them, sometimes clothed, sometimes naked. Sometimes there was what looked like a boy in the corner, curled up in a ball, hands over his head, glowing cigarettes also appeared a lot, being pressed into skin, both of the women and the boy, smoke and swirling lines, scratching out, and monstrous razor-sharp teeth.

Jaq felt ill just imagining the trauma of a child living through everything that he'd seen. She'd thought she'd grown used to depravity in all its forms. She'd rescued children from abusive homes, but this felt like it was on a different level.

She'd seen enough of that thought and flicked through to the trial transcripts. Here she learned exactly how Gregory Black had used his son. She'd heard on the news at the time that Simon had been used as bait, but they had never explained how that was done. This was because

Simon was a minor and the court didn't allow reporting on his part in the crimes.

It turned out that Gregory Black had pushed his son out in front of the women's moving cars. When they came to a halt to check on the injured child, Black would abduct them. While Black had done this awful thing when the women were just setting off and their cars hadn't reached full speed, it nevertheless resulted in numerous fractures to Simon's right arm and ribs, which had all been treated at home. It appeared the only time Simon got to leave the house was at night when his father intended to use him. The boy had also been malnourished, covered in bruises and cigarette burns and vitamin D deficient when he'd been found.

Jaq realised she was gripping the screen so tightly she was in danger of pressing her thumbs right through the monitor, so she forced herself to calm down with some deep breathing and let go of the computer. She was shaking, though. Poor Simon, it was way worse than she's feared. The fact that he'd turned out relatively normal and could hold down a job was a blooming miracle.

There was one more file she wanted to look at, and that was the psychological evaluation. A Doctor Helen Nobel had carried this out. She was quite a good explainer, Jaq discovered, reading through the doctor's notes. Some psychologists were terrible at filling out paperwork about their patients.

From Dr Nobel's notes, Jaq discovered that Simon had tried to kill himself by slitting his wrists, not once but at least twice, while still living with his father. Gregory Black had so cowed his son that he did pretty much everything he was ordered without resistance. He'd also been thoroughly indoctrinated to never trust officialdom and to fear the police. A necessary precaution, Dr Nobel had noted, to protect Black from being betrayed by his son.

The boy had been traumatised and stressed, suffered from insomnia and disassociation. He'd also only ever interacted with his father, so he lacked social skills.

He'd not been taught to read or write either. According to Simon, his father had tried but failed, and forever afterwards referred to Simon as an idiot child. Tests at the institution Simon had been sent to revealed that he had a high IQ but was dyslexic. He learned how to read and write there but it had been a struggle.

Jaq was impressed by the work the young offenders' put into Simon. It was a special unit, reserved for the most troubled kids. Unlike the places where they locked up the less dangerous youths, there had been a lot more therapy and education. Simon had continued to draw, and slowly his work and moved from the images of his trauma to pictures that soothed and calmed.

So that explained the cloud paintings, Jaq thought, and she reached for her wine. Really, the poor kid had suffered more than most. Nothing was his fault, for which Jaq was deeply grateful.

Simon was a survivor. A tenacious one at that. He'd overcome his terrible childhood and become a decent, almost normal adult. Jaq wanted now, more than ever, to get to know the real Simon better. She hoped he'd let her.

15

SIMON WAS CLICKING RAPIDLY through the photos of a returning client's latest furniture release when he came to a picture that grabbed his attention. It was a completely flat daybed with nearly invisible spindly legs and a green velvet base that would blend in well with his current decor.

It would be perfect for Jaq was his first thought, which gave him such a surprise he jerked backwards.

'Is something wrong, boss?' Brian asked, looking up from his job of entering all the client's previous furniture into a picture database.

Aisha also looked up from her task. She was hardworking, but never lost the opportunity to join in any conversation.

'I just found a piece I might buy,' Simon said.

'From these guys?' Aisha said, actually open mouthed in surprise. 'I mean, their cheapest piece is a footstool that costs over a thousand pounds. They aren't good value. I have an uncle who could give you the same thing for a third of the price.'

'You have an uncle for everything,' Brian said, and poked Aisha playfully.

'The price isn't only for the cost of materials.' Since the two apparently wanted to learn from him, Simon was trying his best to explain his world view. Most of the time, the interns seemed to appreciate it. 'Look at this piece and tell me what you see,' Simon said, enlarging the image so that it filled his biggest monitor.

'It's very plain,' Aisha said, 'which I know you like. Elegant design that can tell a story with a single line.'

'It has a perfect balance and will blend in well in my living room.'

'Context is everything,' Brian said, repeating a line Simon had taught him.

'All the same, I didn't realise you earned enough for this kind of furniture,' Aisha said. 'Or have you got a trust fund or lottery winnings or something?'

'Something,' Simon said. 'Now I have my one to one with Sarah. You get on with your work.'

'He's got a flat near the docklands,' Simon heard Brian whisper to Aisha as he left.

'I wonder how much that cost him,' Aisha said, giving Simon a speculative look.

He didn't mind this kind of gossip. His money was honestly earned and he paid his taxes, so he had nothing to worry about. Not on that side, anyway.

He wondered what Sarah would have to tell him, though. She'd finally returned to the office after two weeks, looking paler and thinner.

'Simon,' she said, smiling as he walked into the glass walled meeting room.

'Water,' Simon said, putting down the tray with two glasses and a jug between them.

'Not coffee?'

Her question was valid. Usually, Simon arrived with two mugs of coffee.

'I noticed you were avoiding coffee this morning and looked nauseated when Liz offered you a cup.'

Sarah laughed and said, 'Jaq's observation skills seem to be rubbing off on you.'

'I wouldn't say that, but are you okay?' Simon asked as he settled and got out his iPad. He recorded their meetings instead of taking notes.

'I'm fine. I'm just...' Sarah hesitated, giving Simon a thoughtful once over. 'You won't like hearing this, and for the moment I'd appreciate it if you didn't tell everyone, but I'm pregnant.'

Simon blinked at Sarah, trying to understand why she was giving him this information, till realisation dawned.

'Maternity leave?'

'I've talked it over with Aaron. We're going to share the leave, but overall, I'm going to take a year off.'

'A whole year!'

'I'm sorry,' Sarah said, but her voice held a touch of amusement even while she glanced past Simon to the open plan office beyond.

She was probably looking for anyone listening in. The meeting rooms weren't well soundproofed and Simon realised he'd spoken a bit too loudly.

'Will you come back?'

Simon was well aware that many maternity leaves turned into resignations at the end of the year.

'That is my current plan, but who knows how I'll feel after the baby is born?'

'I see.' It dawned on Simon that his behaviour wasn't entirely appropriate, so he said, 'congratulations,' although he feared it sounded insincere.

Sarah just laughed, flushing happily.

'I've discussed this with Louise and agreed that we'd let you decide whether you want to step up into my role while I'm away. If you don't, then the company will hire a temp.'

Louise was Sarah's line manager. She was an older woman who was easily irritated and Simon was grateful that Sarah had to deal with her. The thought of regular one to ones with Louise was a definite con to stepping up, but he didn't like the idea of an unknown temp as his new line manager either.

'Can I have some time to think about it?'

'Sure, but don't take too long. We need to advertise the position if you aren't interested and that can also take a while.'

Jaq stood outside Simon's house and wondered whether she was being too pushy, especially now that she knew about his life. Then again, if she didn't reach out a hand of friendship, she might never see Simon again. She'd debated the pros and cons till she felt sick of the thoughts that didn't progress past a certain point.

Usually, it was best to avoid damaged people, and yet she still wanted to see Simon. She liked the too thin bastard with the horrifying past. He was everything she should have steered clear of. Everything she'd sworn were massive turn offs. Yet here she was again.

Today she'd gone with Thai. There was no answer to the doorbell, though. Was he ghosting her? Should she take the hint and buzz off?

'Jaq?'

There he was, end of the corridor, only just getting home and not even looking surprised.

'Hello, work do?'

'Schmoozing clients,' he said as he got his key out of his coat pocket. 'What's your excuse?'

'Mainly, I just thought you could use some extra calories.'

Jaq held up a paper bag emblazoned with Siam Dragon in green letters on the front and caressed it lovingly with her right hand like someone showing off a prize on a game show.

'Uh huh.' Simon left the door open behind him as tacit permission for her to enter. 'And the other reasons?'

'Best discussed indoors,' Jaq said, following him in. 'I really should get your mobile number. That way, I can let you know if I'm coming round.' Jaq felt cheeky, but also like if she didn't do this, he wouldn't either. 'And you should give me yours, just... in case.'

'Police harassment,' Simon murmured, but fetched a post it, wrote his number down and pasted it to the dining room table before fetching the plates for their dinner.

It reassured Jaq. He might say one thing, but he was doing another. Maybe he felt the same push pull that she felt.

'Here.' Jaq tore the post-it in two. 'The top number is my personal phone, the bottom's work. I don't expect you to ever need my work number, but just in case.'

Simon nodded and pasted his half of the note on the writing table. Jaq entered his into her phone before she started unpacking the food. The waft of jasmin rice and coconut was nearly intoxicating and her mouth watered.

'Are you on another case?' Simon asked as he handed her a plate, knife and fork.

Jaq decided against telling Simon that they should eat Thai with a fork and spoon, and just scraped half the rice onto her plate.

'I'm afraid so. That's also part of the reason I'm here. Do you want to know about it?'

'No.'

The answer was definite and expected. At least she'd got to know Simon to this extent and with her background check, she understood why he'd be even more reluctant to hear about cases. Especially this one that also involved kids.

'I thought you had to worry about confidentiality,' Simon said, taking a couple of spoonfuls of rice for himself and covering it with the creamy green curry.

'If I call you a consultant, and pay you for your words of wisdom, then I can share certain aspects of the case.'

'Jaq...' Simon said, looking fully at her, which came as a surprise. He seldom held her gaze for long. 'It's really hard for me to hear about other people suffering, especially because of criminal behaviour. Also,' he added, looking back down at his food. 'I really don't know what I can tell you that proper consultants, criminal profilers and psychologists can't. Not to mention your own expertise.'

Jaq nodded and then found herself unable to look at Simon.

'I understand. I... had a proper look at your file. I'm sorry.'

Simon blinked at her and said, 'I assumed you looked at my file a long time ago. It surprised me you came back despite that.'

'Why wouldn't I come back?'

'With my history? Why would you want to go anywhere near me?'

'Because I find you admirable. Because you overcame a dreadful youth and are living a decent life.'

Simon's hand shook and he hastily put his knife down and slipped his hand under the table.

'Sorry,' Jaq said. 'You don't want to talk about that. I just felt I should be honest and tell you what I did. I promise I won't tell another soul about it.'

Simon pursed his lips and gave a long sigh that Jaq couldn't interpret, but then he nodded.

'Let's change the subject,' Jaq said. 'That was all far too heavy and I didn't intend to bring the mood down like this. Tell me about your paintings instead. Why are you so keen on painting the sky?'

'I just think it's beautiful, don't you?' Simon said and looked up to point at one of his meters wide paintings. 'Lots of people, when they're buying a house, want a nice sea view or to overlook a park. But as long as I have a sky view, I'm happy.'

'A sky view?' Jaq tilted her head to consider, thinking about how Simon's only view growing up was somebody's fence. 'Yeah, that does sound pretty good.'

As was the conversation. It was better to talk about nothing in particular, nothing related to work or anybody's sordid past.

'I guess you know about Sarah,' Simon said.

'What should I know?'

'That she's pregnant.'

'Ah, so she told you.'

'She hasn't told everyone else yet, but she's planning her maternity leave and I have to decide what I want to do, so she told me.'

'You don't want her job, do you?'

'I really don't.'

'But it would be extra money and Sarah is involved in the design side, so you'd still be doing what you like.'

'But less of it.'

'So what's the problem?'

Jaq was touched that Simon was using her as a sounding board. It felt, for the first time, like he might be okay with leaning on her a bit. The way she sometimes got support from him, even if he didn't realise it.

Simon shrugged.

'I think I'm less good at adapting to change than I thought. I don't want a new manager, but I also don't want to report directly to Sarah's manager. We don't get on very well.'

'You never know, you might get on well with the new manager.'

Simon looked dubious.

'Maybe.'

'Do you actually have a choice? I mean, if Sarah decides not to go back, you'll have to adapt to that too. What other option do you have?'

'I could just quit the day job and focus on my painting. Maybe even paint something other than clouds,' Simon said with a meaningful look at Jaq.

'Would that be enough to pay the bills?'

'I could do it.'

Jaq stared thoughtfully at Simon, who seemed deep in his own musings.

'No, that would not be good.'

Her sudden forcefulness surprised Simon, and he looked up.

'Why wouldn't it be good?'

'Because you'd be alone. You don't even go away for holidays. It would be really, really bad for you to be holed up in this place day after day, fading away into nothingness.'

Simon's astonishment grew as he listened to Jaq and he said, sounding only slightly defensive, 'What makes you think I'd fade away?'

'Because you'd probably stop eating. I'm convinced you only eat when you're surrounded by people. And I know you've told me you're perfectly happy on your own, but I can't see it being good for you, seriously.'

Simon was looking ever more astonished and Jaq suddenly felt embarrassed and like she'd overstepped another boundary. After all, they weren't even friends, although she felt like they were getting closer. 'I shouldn't nag. I'll change the subject.'

'Again?' Simon said, but didn't pause before he added, 'Sarah told me you were looking for a boyfriend and it wouldn't be Rob.'

Why that comment now, Jaq wondered?

'Oh, she did, did she? Well, she's not wrong, obviously. I felt that if there were still one or two singletons like me, I was okay. But now, I'm the last.'

'I see.'

'Have you ever thought about having kids?'

Simon looked up, puzzled for a second, then his face went white and his fork fell from suddenly nerveless fingers and clattered onto the table, spilling food everywhere.

'No,' Simon muttered, trying to pick up a grain of rice with a hand that was shaking so hard he couldn't get a grip and sent an adjoining pea flying off the table. 'No, no, no, I...I.'

'Simon!' Jaq infused her voice with the imperative they'd trained her in for accidents or aftermaths of violent crimes, to be used on anyone going into shock. 'It's okay. Take a deep breath, and count with me. One!' she said and took a breath.

Simon looked stricken, and she wondered what had triggered him. Whatever it was, it was probably best left unexplored.

'Two!'

This time he followed her and took a deep breath, and followed it with a third, fourth and fifth. It seemed he was familiar with this calming tactic and slowly flushed, embarrassment taken over.

'Do... do you want to have a child?' Simon asked.

'I don't,' Jaq said, keeping it brief, and less surprised that he'd asked than somebody else might be.

She had already noticed that Simon reciprocated. Unlike many men when asked about their holiday, work or hobbies, and who went on at length assuming everyone wanted to know, and stopped when they were done, or switched to talking about something else about their glorious selves, Simon knew the world didn't revolve around him. He knew people liked to be asked about themselves, and so he asked. It made for a refreshing change.

'You don't?' Simon said.

Jaq assumed that as long as the question wasn't about him he could cope, since he'd been fine talking about Sarah's pregnancy too.

'I guess my job has put me off. I've seen what happens to kids,' Jaq said, realising this was probably a mistake, since Simon had been used and abused. 'And I've seen what some kids turn into. Not all, obviously. But also, I like my job, and I don't want to lose out on a decade of experience while my work takes second place to child rearing, which would inevitably happen.'

'Maybe your husband...' Simon said, still shaken but getting calmer.

'Child rearing, done properly, should involve both parents. My feeling is if you're doing it properly, both your careers will be affected. I don't believe the story of having a successful career and bringing up children. It's a big job if you intend to do it right. Besides, you've seen the hours I keep. It would be impossible, right?'

'I guess so.'

'Sorry,' Jaq said, reaching across the table, but not touching Simon. 'I didn't mean for this conversation to get so heavy. Why don't you tell me something else, like... what kinds of shows you enjoy watching?'

Simon gave her a wry smile and said, 'I'm pretty eclectic. I like lots of things. The only stuff I avoid are thrillers and cop shows.'

'Really? Those are the two favourite genres of most of my male friends.'

'Yeah, the guys at work too,' Simon said and, unusually for him, helped himself to a second serving of food, this time the mango and coconut sticky rice dessert. 'But I find them too stressful. How about you?'

'I hate cop shows too,' Jaq said and, as with everyone else she'd ever told, it surprised Simon.

'You don't like cop shows?'

'They drive me crazy with their appalling policing. All the bullshit in-fighting between colleagues, and the disregard for laws and correct police procedure, some of which is downright vigilantism. And don't even get me started on the stupid plots. For instance, the only two cops I ever knew who were accused of a crime really did it. Most criminals are far too stupid to successfully frame a cop, and serial killers, they aren't omniscient super criminals, they—'

Jaq stopped dead. She'd gone and done it again and Simon had frozen, watching her uncertainly.

'Sorry, I completely forgot.'

'Really?' Simon said warily. 'I guess... that's a good thing.'

'I have never conflated you with Gregory Black. If I had, there's no way I'd sleep over.'

'No... I don't suppose you would.'

'You know, it's been a weird night, but not altogether bad. Maybe we're getting more comfortable with each other, and that's why all the stuff we've never dared touch upon has started coming out.'

Although thinking about it, Jaq was the one poking all of Simon's sensitive spots. Her life had been textbook boring middle class, except maybe her sensitivity about boyfriends, but it hardly compared.

Simon looked like he was considering her statement. He'd tilted his head to the side and was absentmindedly poking his last piece of mango. Jaq decided against pushing him. She'd come mainly because she'd wanted to see him, but she was also tired and a monstrous yawn overwhelmed her.

'You should go to sleep,' Simon said.

'I really should.' Jaq decided she'd be graceful about Simon's obvious wish to wrap things up. 'The station has finished the overnight room renovations. I should get going.'

'If you want…' Simon started and then stopped.

'Are you actually offering me your damned uncomfortable sofa?'

Simon flushed and said, 'I bought a daybed.'

'A what?' Jaq asked, glancing across at the living room area that was now shrouded in darkness.

Simon whisked up his phone, fiddled with it for a moment, and a standard lamp and pair of wall sconces came on, washing the room in a soft glow. That was when Jaq realised the half of the sitting room that had been occupied by Simon's giant easel now held an elegant flat stretch of olive green velvet daybed. It was a perfect single bed with two pillow-like cushions at either end.

'The blanket,' Simon said, handing it over. 'And a sheet for the sofa.'

'You bought this for me?'

'Of course not.' Simon turned his back on her so she couldn't see his face. 'I just liked the look of it.'

'Sure you did,' Jaq said and wondered what was really happening here.

'You seem cheerful today, Simon,' Liz said as she dropped off his coffee at his desk.

It was her turn to do the team drinks and she was making her usual slow rounds, stopping to gossip at each table.

'Yeah.'

'Looks like you've gained some weight, too. Well done.'

Simon felt too embarrassed to reply and merely gave her a smile before taking a sip of coffee. Fortunately, Liz didn't expect him to gossip and moved on.

'It's because of Jaq, isn't it?' Sarah said, leaning across her chair to close the gap between them. 'She told me she's been going round to yours lately.'

It appalled Simon to know that Jaq had told anybody about her visits. Not that they amounted to much. Just Jaq turning up with food, a bit of chat and her falling asleep, usually vanishing the next morning if not sooner and without a word being exchanged. It was odd how on her last visit he'd slept better with her in the house.

His dismay must have been reflected on his face because Sarah just gave him a smile and said, 'Don't worry, she's only told me and I won't tell anybody else.'

Simon sincerely hoped that would be the case.

'Have you had any thoughts on the other matter?'

Simon nodded. 'I talked it over with Jaq.'

'Did you now? And what did she say?'

'That life is change.'

'I'll bet she had you doing most of the talking. I guess because of her work, I often find myself divulging more than I'd intended to Jaq. But usually it's helpful to talk things through.'

Simon tried to think back to the conversation. His memory was blurred, shaken by some parts of the conversation. He dismissed talking to Sarah about the possibility of resignation, the one thing Jaq had been adamant about.

Simon checked they couldn't be overheard and said, 'You should get a temp. Even if I act up, you'd have to get one to replace my post, anyway.'

'Okay,' Sarah said. 'I'll tell Louise.'

'I hope you do come back,' Simon said.

16

Simon stared at his phone, trying to make sense of the message. It was from Jaq. The first time she'd messaged him. He was on the work group chat, and got the occasional work related text, but this was something new.

I'm going to Brighton this Saturday. Do you fancy joining me? You'd get to see the sea!

As far as he was concerned, the exclamation mark was unnecessary. And what he was most curious about in Brighton was the pavilion. That was a must, whether you thought it a masterpiece, an interesting curiosity or a design disaster.

Simon regretted opening the message. Now Jaq would know he'd read it. He also couldn't stop double checking his phone, as if there'd been a mistake and Jaq would recall the text.

'Oh, so she's messaging you, is she?' Rob said, reading over Simon's shoulder.

Simon was so surprised he nearly dropped the phone.

'I heard you two broke up.'

'Well...' Rob's face scrunched into a disgruntled grimace, 'according to her, we hadn't really started dating.'

'Oh,' Simon said, uncertain of what to add.

He rarely engaged in talk about lovers, partners, marital feuds or kids, since he had nothing to contribute.

'I told her she was wasting her time with you.'

Simon blinked at Rob, trying to understand the significance of the words.

'The two of you talked about me?'

'I saw you guys hanging out at the art expo. I could tell she fancied you.'

'She does?' Simon said, and he started feeling panicky.

'Half the women in this office have had a crush on you at one time or another,' Rob said, waving his hand to encompass all the people at their desks.

'They have?'

Rob laughed so loudly it made the people closest to them jump.

'I guess you didn't realise. Typical. That's exactly why I told Jaq not to bother with you. So, are you going to go to Brighton with her?'

'I don't know,' Simon said, but his not very strong competitive spirit was surging and he thought he might, after all.

'She's a forceful woman, probably more than you can handle,' Rob said, patting Simon's shoulder. 'Just do what you feel comfortable with.'

Simon nodded, feeling less inclined than ever to follow Rob's advice as he watched him stroll away, stopping to talk to Aisha. He had a habit of chatting up all the new women in the office.

'He's just jealous,' Sarah said, leaning around their dividing board. 'Ignore him.'

'I was planning to.'

Sarah gave him a beaming smile and said, 'I think you and Jaq could have a good time. Why not try it?'

So now Simon had two conflicting pieces of advice. And thinking about what he'd say meant he could barely concentrate on his work. His initial reaction had been an immediate no. But then he'd wavered and that was a surprise.

Aside from going to work, he rarely left the haven of his flat. He'd barely seen much of London aside from visiting clients and the occasional team building day. His least favourite had been paint balling in an outer London brownfield site full of paint splattered, half demolished buildings and scratchy scrub.

He'd found running, hiding and trying not to get shot, far too stressful. He was relieved when he got caught in the crossfire between his red team and the blue team. It meant he could go back to the tented base and wile away the day with the rest of the physically and mentally incompetent while comparing bruises.

His favourite, unexpectedly, had been a day of helping at an urban farm. Aside from seeing other people's cats and dogs, he'd not come across any other animals. The size and smell of cows, pigs, sheep and goats had astonished him, as had the aggression of the roosters and the geese.

Dirty as the work of cleaning out stalls had been, though, he'd enjoyed it. He still had a standing order giving the farm a monthly donation, although he'd not been back. The farm had no CCTV.

I'll wear a body cam if that makes you more comfortable, said a message from Jaq when Simon was packing up to go home. *I promise we'll have fun.*

Simon wasn't convinced, but he'd had enough therapy in his life to know his hesitation meant he was at least interested. Whether that was for the pavilion, the sea, or to spend some time with Jaq was still undecided.

OK, he messaged, *but I want to see the pavilion.*

Your wish is my command! Let's meet at Croydon Station at 10am. We need an early start if we're going to get all the Brighton sightseeing done in a day.

Simon stared at the phone, thinking he'd lost his mind. He hadn't even confirmed the body cam. It was stupid, but it probably would have made him feel safer. Only Dr Nobel had asked him to try to overcome this anxiety, so he'd said nothing. Not about that or about going out in a twosome with an attractive woman.

17

I T WAS AN INDICATION of how well she'd got to know Simon that Jaq first looked for the CCTV at Croydon Station. Sure enough, Simon was standing in full view of the camera, watching the entry gates like a hawk, in a surprisingly bright long sleeved, red t-shirt.

It was a bit of a faff to get Poppy through the barriers, retrievers were always such eager dogs. Jaq regretted not taking her for an early walk before heading off. The advantage was that the crowd moved aside to let Poppy through.

'Simon!' Jaq said in her getting somebody's attention voice and then she waved as he turned to find her.

She felt like she was grinning from ear to ear, but didn't know what to do as she got close. A hug would be too much, a handshake too weird. So she just gave him a nod.

'You have a dog,' Simon said and took a step back as Poppy tried to sniff his leg.

'Not mine. She's the reason I'm going to Brighton. I'm returning her to my aunt. My parents have been dog sitting while aunt's been on holiday.'

'Oh,' Simon said, and he looked uncertain.

'Shit, I didn't think to ask. You're not allergic or phobic or anything, are you?' Jaq said, reeling Poppy's lead in so that she was pinned to Jaq's side.

'No, I... like animals,' Simon said, although he sounded unsure.

Jaq assumed he had little experience with them.

'Come on, let's get on the train. Then we can chat and I'll introduce you properly to Poppy.'

They didn't have long to wait for the regular Brighton service and were lucky to get a four seat configuration, so they landed up facing each other with Poppy taking up the floor between them. She was sitting in her, I'm very happy to meet you, and curious about you, pose, one ear cocked.

'What is she?' Simon said as he leaned forward and held his hand out, but at a safe distance.

Poppy leaned in for a sniff and then gave Simon's hand a thorough licking. He flinched, but didn't back away.

'She's a springer spaniel, very friendly, as you can see, and far too energetic to live in a tiny house in Brighton. At least my aunt takes her for loads of walks.'

'I suppose so,' Simon said and glanced around the carriage.

Jaq guessed he was looking for the cameras and checking out the other passengers. The carriage was half full, which was quite empty for the Brighton train on a Saturday in the summer. Presumably it would fill as the morning progressed. In the meantime, they'd left the griminess of Croydon behind and were into the Green Belt of rolling hills, fields, hedgerows and copses of oak and ash.

'It's pretty, isn't it? I'm always amazed at how lush everything looks in the summer, with hardly a cloud in the sky today. You'll see Brighton at its best.'

'Yeah,' Simon said, gazing out the window, 'that will be good.'

He looked more relaxed than usual and Jaq left him to take in the scenery. After all, it was probably a novelty to him, which was a shame. Jaq was biased, but the English countryside seemed like one of the loveliest places on Earth to her.

With so much to take in, the forty-five minute journey seemed to be over in a flash as they pulled into the large, Victorian station.

'Poppy knows she's nearly home,' Jaq said, holding the excited dog back as they made their way down the platform and through the station.

'So... we're going to your aunt's house first?' Simon said, walking alongside Jaq.

'Yeah, I mainly invited you so you could see the sea. But I also brought you along to keep my aunt from chatting to me for the rest of the day. That woman can talk for England.'

'Ah.'

'It isn't far. We can walk there. To be fair, you can pretty much walk to anywhere in Brighton. If you don't mind walking.'

'I don't mind,' Simon said, scanning the road and then followed Jaq as she took a left and they walked down a steep narrow road and then took another left.

'It's so seasidey, isn't it?' Jaq said of the row of tiny terrace houses painted in a rainbow array of pastels, the gardens filled with beach pebbles and spiky blue grey seaside plants, side by side with roses and towering hollyhocks.

'I suppose so,' Simon said, and at least he appeared fascinated by what he was seeing.

Jaq hoped that the artist in him found this diversity interesting. She stopped in front of a sunshine yellow house, made her way up the short path to the marine blue door and rang the brass ship's bell, all so cliched it was embarrassing. Poppy was already whining in anticipation, then broke into excited yips at the sound of her aunt clattering her way to the door.

'Poppy!' Gloria said, holding her arms out wide and the dog leapt up, giving a series of ear shattering yips and licked her aunt's face. 'And Jaq, of course,' Gloria said, staying crouched down and massaging Poppy's velvety soft ears. 'Come in for some tea.'

'Ah, I'd love to, but I can't.' Jaq reached back to where Simon was lurking and gently pulled him forward. 'This is my friend Simon, who's never been to Brighton. I promised to show him all the sights.'

'Hello,' Simon said and held his hand out.

'Simon, hey?' Gloria said, looking him up and down as she gave his hand a thorough pumping. 'I've never met one of Jaq's gentlemen friends before.'

'Honestly, so old-fashioned,' Jaq said, rolling her eyes. 'Simon's an artist.'

'Oh, then he must go to the Pavilion.'

'It's on our list.'

'Along with the pier, and fish and chips on the beach. Frightfully overpriced, but worth it.'

'Exactly, so I'll leave you to fawn over Poppy, and we'll be off. I'm sure you're still recuperating from your trip, too.'

'I most certainly am. Morocco was fantastic, but far too hot to visit in summer. I'll tell you all about it next time. I wouldn't want to cramp your style by being a third wheel,' Gloria said, giving an exaggerated wink.

'This is why I love you so much. You know exactly what I'm thinking and you're so diplomatic.'

Gloria laughed, blew kisses to Jaq and Simon and watched as they hurried away.

'It's only a ten-minute walk to the beach from here,' Jaq said. 'but I'll take you via the Lanes. No need to buy anything, but I love all the quirky little shops. It's all very hippy and filled with the scent of incense and dope.'

'And that doesn't bother you?'

'I put my police instincts aside when I'm wandering the Lanes. There are loads of great jewellery shops which I focus on. The colourful and baggy clothes made from hemp might be comfortable, but not really something I can wear to work.'

Simon nodded and looked around, taking in the narrow lane that was filled with dawdling shoppers. It always felt so relaxed and slow compared to London.

'What do you think?' Jaq said, making a beeline for a tray of silver rings.

'It's interesting.'

Jaq wondered whether Simon was enjoying himself. His facial expression always gave the impression of somebody absorbed in their own thoughts and seldom changed. So she glanced down at his hands. At least they weren't shaking. In fact, he looked calm.

'And there's the sea,' Jaq said, waving down a wider avenue they'd just turned into. 'Not spectacular yet, but wait till we get closer. I'll take you all the way to the end of the pier so you can experience its full magnificence.'

'Okay,' Simon said, with his gaze fixed on the silvery line of the sea in the distance.

At least he looked more interested now. Jaq wished he'd tell her what he thought, but he was probably used to keeping things to himself and since she'd already talked him into going out for the day, she decided not to push him for more.

'The famous Brighton Pier,' Jaq said as they passed under the arch of circus like lights and strolled down the wide wooden promenade.

There were shops all the way down the middle of the pier and funfair rides at the end. Jaq took hold of Simon's hand, earning her a surprised look, and walked him briskly through the crowds to the end.

'Tada!' Jaq said, flinging her arms out wide. 'The sea! Or rather, the Atlantic Ocean.'

'It's big.'

Simon leaned out over the railings, taking in the choppy, blueish grey ocean, blue skies with towering clouds above and a flock of seagulls screeching overhead. Then he pulled his phone out of his jeans pocket and took a series of snaps.

'Will that provide you with inspiration?'

'Definitely.'

Simon turned his back to the sea and took a bunch of shots of the fairground and the sky above.

'Hello, gorgeous,' a well built but oily looking man said, grinning broadly as he strolled over.

He was wearing a sleeveless t-shirt designed to show off his muscles. A younger, ginger lad with severe acne accompanied him, along with an even younger blond kid. Jaq turned her back on them, determined to not let anything spoil her day. But the muscle bound man wasn't going to be got rid of so easily.

'Hey, don't be rude,' he said, coming around to face her again.

'Back off,' Simon said in the same quiet voice he always spoke in as he stepped in front of Jaq.

'Oh look at this,' Muscles said. 'You protecting your girlfriend, twig man?'

'No, I'm protecting you.'

Aside from being astonished that he'd stepped in, Jaq was also interested to note that Simon wasn't nervous, and projected quite an intimidating air. What he said also surprised Muscles, who took an involuntary step back.

'He's right,' Jaq said in her best police, controlling the situation, voice. She was more than capable of dealing with these three. 'So, if you don't want any trouble, I suggest you stop here.'

Apparently, facing two implacable, unfazed people did the job. Muscles spat on the boardwalk and indicated with his head for his cronies to follow.

'Well, that was unexpected,' Jaq said as the trio disappeared amongst the crowd.

'What was?' Simon asked.

'You stepping in. I'm sorry to say that getting harassed by men is a fairly common occurrence.'

'That's because you're attractive,' Simon said and strolled away, back down the pier.

Jaq realised she was staring at him, mouth open. She snapped it shut and hurried after him. So he thought she was attractive. That was good to know. Although it would have been nice if he'd said it with some enthusiasm.

'Ok, let's get lunch and eat it on the beach. Fish and chips is traditional, but not mandatory,' Jaq said as she hurried to catch up with Simon.

'I quite like fish and chips, although I've only ever had it in pubs.'

'I think you'll like this version,' Jaq said as they made their way off the pier and down the steps to the beachfront, that was lined with shops as far as the eye could see.

Every second beachside shop was selling fish and chips and ice cream, the rest specialised in beach towels, seaside memorabilia and paintings of varying degrees of talent. Simon was drawn to the paintings while Jaq headed for her favourite fish and chips joint.

They bought a faux newspaper cone of chips each, and another with the battered fish. Then they hobbled their way across the Brighton shingle, dodging playing children and working their way around families who'd staked out their areas with colourful towels, sun umbrellas and cool bags of food and drink. They finally reached a reasonably isolated spot where they could take in the waves washing onto the shore, tumbling the shingle forward then back.

'This is the life,' Jaq said with a satisfied sigh as she settled into a sunny hollow.

She pegged a chip with the accompanying wooden fork and savoured the crispy salt and vinegar outside and the fluffy, creamy inside. Simon watched her for a bit, then tucked in and turned to gazing out to sea.

Once she'd taken the edge off her hunger, Jaq said, 'Thanks for standing up for me on the pier.'

'It was nothing,' Simon said, and looked like he really meant it.

'Really? It made me see you in a different light. Forgive me for saying this, because it's my bias. But until today, I'd only seen you as a victim. After that encounter, I realised you're tougher than I thought.'

'Not really,' Simon said, keeping his head down and looking like he was trying to decide which chip to eat next.

'Yes, really,' Jaq said. 'It takes courage to stand up to people.'

'They weren't dangerous,' Simon muttered, turning red. 'I can at least tell the difference between the ones that can and will inflict harm and the ones that are full of hot air.'

'All the same. It takes real mental fortitude to get over a shitty childhood. You may not think so, but you've done really well.'

Simon glanced around at the other people on the beach, verified that they were out of earshot, and then gave Jaq another noncommittal shrug.

'Do you mind if I ask you a few things about your life? I don't mean to pry. Think of it as getting to know a friend. But if I ask anything uncomfortable, just answer, no comment. Would that be okay?'

Simon glanced at her dubiously but nodded and said, 'Okay, ask.'

'What's your favourite colour?'

'Blue,' Simon said without hesitation. 'All the shades from nearly white to inky blue black.'

'See, that wasn't so hard, was it?'

'No, but you're a trained interrogator. You probably always start out with something easy,' Simon said as he broke off a piece of fish and chewed it thoughtfully.

'Is it good?'

'Very.'

'For the record, this isn't an interrogation, although all the men in my life have accused me of interrogating them. I wasn't. I just wanted to know them better.'

Simon looked over at her, shading his eyes as the sun was behind her.

'Am I a man in your life?'

'Very much so,' Jaq said, pleased that he'd asked. 'Next question. Have you ever owned a pet?'

'No.'

'But you like animals.'

'In as much as I know them, I suppose I do.'

'Getting a pet would probably be good for you. A cat, not a dog. Dogs are pack animals and hate being alone. It stresses them too much. But a cat would provide you with company.'

'I'm perfectly fine on my own.'

'Even introverts gain comfort from company.'

Simon looked dubious, but ate a chip instead of disagreeing.

'I'm assuming you're an extrovert. Do you have a pet?'

'I probably am an extrovert. But I don't have a pet. Growing up, we always had pets, cats and dogs, and my parents still do, but I'm not home enough even for a cat.'

It pleased Jaq that this was turning into a decent two way conversation. It wasn't the way she'd expected things to go, considering how silent Simon had been until now. Then again, he'd probably been absorbing everything.

'Do you have any friends?'

Simon turned back to her briefly and then turned to studying the ceaseless waves, a considering frown etching into his brow.

'Probably not.'

'Do you feel like elaborating?'

Without withdrawing his eyes from the waves, he said, 'I was too much of a mess when I first arrived at the young offenders'. I don't remember a lot about my first year. In the second year, I started to settle down, but I had so much to figure out and overcome that I didn't engage with the other guys. To be fair, I didn't actually know how to make friends and they weren't the type of guys you'd want as friends, anyway. A whole lot of them were never going to leave, or were going to be hidden away upon release with a name change, like me, so impossible to hang out with. Not that Dr Nobel would have wanted me to, anyway.'

'Your psychiatrist,' Jaq said.

'Is she mentioned in my records?'

'She is. She said you'd adapted well to the world when you were introduced into it.'

'I'm glad she thinks so. I mean, I don't think she's totally wrong. I am doing okay.'

'And afterwards? You went to art college.'

'Yeah,' Simon said, and he gave a slight introspective smile that reassured Jaq because he'd been looking rather sombre up till now. 'I was terrified in my first year. Just going outside during the day was a challenge, and hanging out with all those artistic kids was kind of terrifying. I kept to myself the first year, but artists are a strange bunch, extroverts and introverts, easy going, insecure or massive egos. It was probably a good place for me to start because they didn't consider me any weirder than anybody else. And with Dr Nobel's help, I figured out how to get involved in group projects and going to parties and being able to have conversations.'

'But you didn't make friends?'

'I kind of did. When they have a party, or an art show, I go along.'

'Always in a group.'

Simon nodded, laid his half eaten food on the ground beside himself and picked up a smooth creamy stone, hefting it in one hand mediately.

'You know why. Some of the girls invited me out on... I guess they were dates, but I never went.'

'And then you went to work.'

'At London Marketing. It's the first company I've ever worked at and I'm comfortable with them.'

'But you've never gone out with just one of them either.'

Simon shook his head.

'I didn't dare to. You may think it's foolish, but that's because you don't have my past. Anything I do will be seen through the lens of my record. You can say I was a victim too, but how quickly would that turn to considering that my childhood drove me to become a rapist and murderer?'

'It isn't fair, I know,' Jaq said, popping her last piece of fish into her mouth. 'But I'm afraid you're right. After I saw you had a record, it made it more justifiable to haul you in when Liz disappeared. I'm sorry about that.'

Simon shrugged.

'It freaked me out, but it also confirmed my bias.'

'Which is why I'm particularly pleased that you came out with me today,' Jaq said, leaning over to Simon's half-eaten piece of fish and giving him a questioning look. He waved his hand to indicate she could take it. 'I'm glad you trusted me enough to take this leap of faith. Thank you.'

Simon blushed and turned his head so Jaq couldn't see his face.

'Just make sure you get home safely, that's all I ask.'

18

'I WENT TO BRIGHTON with Jaq,' Simon said the moment he sat down in Dr Nobel's office.

'Just the two of you?' Helen asked, and she looked surprised but also pleased.

'Yeah. She texted me once she got home so I know she's okay,' Simon said, flushing to admit, albeit obliquely, how nervous he'd been until he'd received the text.

'How was the outing?'

'Good,' Simon said as he recalled bits of the day. 'I saw the sea. It's... big and constantly on the move.'

Simon looked up to see that Dr Nobel was grinning at him.

'I'm glad you had that experience, both of them. I assume I can safely say it was your first date. Am I right?'

'Do all the takeaways at mine not count?'

'Probably not as an official date. Although you were getting to know each other through that. So now the big question, what do you want to do next?'

Simon's leg started to jump, so he put his hand firmly on it to keep it still.

'You mentioned CBT the last time we met, but I'm not sure... I don't think it will be enough.'

'Why do you think that, Simon?'

'Um...' Now his hands were shaking too and his leg had gone back to bouncing. 'This happened a while ago. One of the times Jaq came to my house.'

Simon stopped again. This was so hard to bring up, he almost felt on the very of a panic attack.

'Deep breaths, Simon,' Dr Noble said, her voice calm and non judgemental as always. 'Just take deep breaths and speak when you're ready.'

He didn't feel ready, not at all. He actually wanted to jump up and run away. But this was something he had to work through because it was troubling him more each day.

'So... J.j.j.jaq asked me if I wanted to have kids. I mean, in the distant future, hypothetically.'

'I understand.'

'But the moment she said it, I... I thought about how babies are made... you know, sex,' the last word came out as a whisper and now Simon had his gaze fixed on the carpet because he was too ashamed to look up into Dr Nobel's eyes. 'I had this... this vivid image popped into my head of the two of us, naked but... I had my hands wrapped about her throat, ch.choking her.'

Simon breathed out, relieved and ashamed that he'd revealed this secret.

'I see,' Helen said, still in that same, half disinterested voice. 'It's understandable.'

'Is it? I was so shocked I froze up.'

'It's something I should have considered before. I'm sorry I didn't. This is going to be a tough question for you to answer but, have you ever seen anyone else other than your father having sex?'

'What?'

'Do you ever watch porn?'

'No,' Simon said, looking up at Dr Nobel to try to understand what she was thinking to even ask this question. 'Gregory Black watched porn all the time. It was disgusting.'

'As I recall, his porn stash was all on the sadistic side,' Helen said. 'And most certainly illegal, too. I'm not surprised it repulsed you.'

Simon nodded and tried to get some control over his shaking.

'But you know, Gregory Black wasn't normal, Simon.'

'I know.'

'What you probably aren't aware of is that people habituate to what they see. If you only see sex the way you did, you'll think that's the only way sex happens, and seeing something similar may arouse you in the future.'

Simon shuddered at the very idea.

'I don't want that.'

'Okay, so I think, what we need to do before the CBT is a bit of sex ed.'

'I know what it is,' Simon said, embarrassed that at his age, they were talking about something like this.

'But I'd like you to consider looking at this,' Helen said as she rummaged around in her drawer and then took out a small, black thumb drive. 'A sex therapist colleague of mine produced this. It's an explanation, with videos, showing what healthy, consensual sex should look like. I'm afraid too many people get their ideas about sex from porn, which isn't necessarily the best role model. Do you think you'd be okay with watching this?'

The idea repulsed Simon. Of course, he was aware that most people didn't do what his father had done, especially to the point of death, but he'd never dwelled too deeply on it lest he became overcome by lust. Something he feared more than being hauled off by the police because he wasn't sure what kind of monster he'd turn into. But if he was going to overcome this, and not have his imagination lead him into such dark places, he was going to have to do something.

'I'll try.'

'Good for you,' Helen said as she came out from behind her desk and handed the drive over. 'Take your time, don't push yourself and if it is too hard to watch on your own, we can solve this problem in another way, okay?'

Simon nodded and made a pathetic attempt at a smile.

'This is a huge step,' Helen said. 'Don't underestimate it or yourself. You've come a long way in a short period. I'm so proud of you.'

Simon felt himself blushing. He shouldn't have been so happy to be praised like this, but it made him feel like a kid being told he was a good boy by his mother. It was so utterly different to when colleagues praised his work, which he could take with a slight smile and nod, gratified but not overwhelmed.

19

—·—

SIMON PUT A DAB of paint on his latest work and
glanced out of the window. He always pulled the
curtains right back when he was painting to maximise
light. It was a pleasant day, with a deep blue sky and
towering fluffy clouds. He'd already stopped a couple of
times to take photos for future paintings.

He hadn't quite got used to painting in his room and
wondered, yet again, why he'd really bought the daybed.
It really was as if he wanted Jaq to stay over. Or at least,
he wanted her to be comfortable when she did stay over.
Which was odd. He should have been making it less
comfortable to ensure she stayed away.

That set his hand to shaking with the combined fear of
never seeing her again, and seeing her. Or worse, having to
decide, one way or another, whether he wanted to see her.
It was something he hadn't been able to decide yet, not
helped by Jaq's absence. It had been two weeks since he'd
seen her and he'd had nothing since, not even a text.

So far, even his therapy hadn't helped him decide what
to do. But he'd started on CBT to allow him to feel more
comfortable touching women. The video of consensual
sex had surprised him because it felt so normal and
ordinary, but it was still too difficult to watch and he'd had

to stop halfway and confess as much to Dr Nobel. So she's stepped back and these days his homework was to watch a daily half hour of people kissing from a video Dr Nobel had given him.

He squirmed as he watched. His emotions seesawing between panic, nausea and desire. What was worse was that the kissing images kept popping into his head throughout the day, making it hard to focus on his work. He should probably mention it to Dr Nobel. Maybe they were still moving too quickly.

The doorbell went off, jerking Simon out of his introspection. It had to be Jaq. This thought set his heart to racing and made his palms sweaty.

He wiped his brush clean and snapped the lids shut on his paints, but he was too slow and she rang the bell again. She was certainly an impatient woman. He planned to say that as he opened the door. Only he was facing a really pale, usually grim Jaq.

'Are you okay?'

Jaq walked slap bang up to him, rested her forehead on his chest and mumbled, 'Horrible case. Kids stabbing another kid.'

'Shit... I'm sorry.'

'It's over now. We got them. And the mastermind. You were right, when you said there was more behind the Brad Davis case than we realised. We've been following it up ever since. Remember the case you didn't want to hear about?'

'Yeah,' Simon said, feeling guilty now that he'd been so clear with his refusal.

'Well, this person was behind that as well. And this latest one. I can't go into detail, but without your hunch, we might never have connected the three cases. So... I just thought you should know, you were a big help.'

'Ah... that's good,' Simon said, wondering what he did now, because Jaq's head was still plastered to his chest.

'I feel bloody awful,' Jaq mumbled.

'Go inside, then, get some sleep.'

Simon noted Jaq hadn't even bothered to turn up with food. Nor had the team gone out for a boozy celebration after finishing a case. Both spoke volumes.

'I can't sleep. I haven't slept in days, but I can't, not yet.'

'I understand.'

Simon knew all about trauma induced shock, but he also knew something that could help. He stepped away from Jaq and left her swaying in place, her gaze fixed on the floor.

He rummaged in the hall cupboard, pulled out a blanket, fetched a couple of cushions and said, 'Come on, let's go.'

'Where to?'

'You'll see.'

Simon took a firm hold of Jaq's hand, even though it made him jumpy and pulled her out of the flat.

'Seriously, though?'

'Don't worry, we're not going far,' Simon said and led Jaq upstairs.

'The rooftop?' Jaq asked.

'Yeah, come on, it's not much further.'

Simon headed for the centre of the building, where there was a concrete block with a slightly inclined metal roof on top of it.

He flapped the blanket out, dropped the cushions at the high end and said, 'Sit.'

'On the blanket?'

'Where else?' Simon fetched a faded old red umbrella that was propped up against the stairwell wall and opened it so that it cast shade over their faces but didn't obscure their view of the sky. 'Don't worry, you're safe with me,' Simon said as he sat down beside her.

He wanted to reassure Jaq, but he wasn't sure if what he said was remotely helpful. Either way, Jaq seemed too tired to care and settled on the blanket, looking around, not taking much in.

'Now, lie down,' Simon said, lay uphill and tucked his hands under his head. 'And look up.'

Jaq did as ordered and lay blinking up into the blue, cloud dabbed sky fringed by the scallop-edged umbrella.

'Nice,' she murmured.

'Sky therapy,' Simon said as an emotion he didn't understand welled up inside him.

He was probably just glad he could help, he decided.

'You and your skies,' Jaq said, but at least she smiled.

So now Simon knew for sure he'd done the right thing.

'Just empty your mind. Think of nothing but the clouds drifting by.'

Jaq nodded, gazed skywards, took a deep breath, and slowly let it out. It seemed some of her tension went with it. Simon did the same, watching as high unseen winds pushed the clouds along at surprising speed so that they drifted and uncurled, swirled and reformed into new shapes.

He felt Jaq's fingers brush against his hand and curl around his little finger and ring finger. It gave him a shock and an instant sensation of combined pleasure and fear. He tilted his head to look at Jaq. Her eyes were closed and her breathing was deep and regular. She was dropping off to sleep.

Simon considered pulling his hand free. But he didn't want to wake Jaq and... a part of him, jangling nerves and all, didn't want to let go either.

So he decided to treat it like CBT and try to get used to it. When that got too difficult, he switched to ignoring the touch and let his mind wander over the time he'd got to know Jaq. It really was quite astonishing how she'd pushed herself into his life. He'd had no intention of letting anybody in and yet here he was outside, not a camera in sight, with a woman who also spent the occasional night at his house.

The fact that she did sometimes filled him with terror. He often thought he should ask her to stop coming by. So far, he'd not been able to work up the courage.

Maybe today would be a good time. When Jaq woke up. Or maybe not. Maybe he'd just stick with the therapy and see how far he could push himself.

A sensation of being on a rather hard bed woke Jaq, and she blinked up into a sky that was now bright orange, streaked with pink clouds.

'What time is it?'

'Just past eight thirty,' Simon said, sitting up.

He looked anxious, as he often did around her, but also, with his face lit by the glow of sunset, ridiculously handsome. Not for the first time, Jaq felt a warm,

comforting affection billow up for this man. She wished
she saw the same affection reflected on his face. She
supposed for now she'd have to be happy with the small
steps he had taken. At least this thing wasn't all one way.

'I really needed that, thanks,' Jaq said, and stretched her
arms high over her head, cracking her neck. 'Did you stay
with me all day?'

'I did.'

'Did you at least get some sleep?'

Simon shook his head and Jaq wondered whether he'd
stayed awake deliberately. Considering his anxiety, he
probably wouldn't have dared to go to sleep anyhow.

'How about getting up for food? Please tell me you at
least had lunch.'

Jaq would have been ravenous by now. In fact, she was,
but Simon barely ate, and less when he was stressed. She
hoped she hadn't upset him to the point of making him
lose his appetite.

'I didn't eat,' Simon said with a slight, embarrassed
smile. 'You know I'm not a big eater.'

'Good grief, all the same, just a snack or something
would have been good.'

'And leave a woman asleep, up here, all on her own…
No.'

Jaq gave him her speculative detective look that left most
people, Simon included, discomforted.

'It isn't a public area though, is it? Although, I'm
surprised you brought me here, away from all the cameras.'

'That was a risk.'

Jaq had to give Simon kudos for his honesty and his
willingness to say things most people would hide.

'What are you going to do about it now?'

'Make sure you leave in one piece. There are cameras in the carpark that record everyone coming and going in this building. As long as you're recorded there, it should be okay.'

To Jaq, the reasoning verged on laughable, although as a detective, she knew he was right; it would be evidence. It was just that she wished he didn't worry so much.

'I promise to make sure my face is fully visible when I leave and I'll text you again when I get home, okay?'

Simon nodded. It was hard to tell in the setting sun, but it also looked like he'd flushed. So he was embarrassed, which she hadn't intended to do to him. She was sad that their Brighton trip hadn't helped him relax in this kind of situation, but she supposed it was progress that he'd even brought her to this camera free zone.

'Do you think we can order some food now? I'm starving and you must be, too. And even if you aren't, you should eat something.'

'Okay,' Simon said and made to stand up.

'Wait,' Jaq said, taking his hand. 'Do you think they'd deliver to the roof?'

'You want to stay up here?' Simon said, looking down at her grip but not doing anything to remove his hand.

'Oh, sorry,' Jaq said, and let go. 'The weather is glorious, as is the view. Let's have a picnic.'

Simon only hesitated for a second before taking out his phone.

'What do you want to eat?'

'Pizza,' Jaq said without hesitation. 'Bonus is that it doesn't need cutlery.'

'Fair enough,' Simon said and ordered the flavour of the pizza Jaq wanted, making sure they'd bring it to the roof. It seemed it was a place he'd ordered from before.

Jaq zoned out, contemplated offering to pay, then decided, as Simon said nothing, to just leave it. It felt nice to have him buy her food.

'They'll be half an hour,' he said and swivelled back to facing her.

'I'll just about survive that,' Jaq said. 'Sarah tells me you've gone with the temp option.'

'Is there anything you two don't talk about?'

'Very little.'

'But why talk about me?'

Simon sounded both puzzled and slightly irritated.

'Mmm, I wonder?' Jaq gave Simon a mischievous smile. 'Maybe it's because I like you.' The confession surprised Simon so much he snapped round to stare at her. 'Couldn't you tell?' Jaq said, feeling the same level of embarrassment as when she'd confessed to her high school crush.

'I...' Simon said and then tailed off, still just staring.

'You're a good guy, observant and caring. You're handsome and professional in your job. What's not to like?'

'And what about the rest?'

'Your past? I'll admit I struggled with it. But I've got to know you during the time we've spent together. I'm more certain than before that what happened in your past was nothing to do with you. Given your personality, it must have been really hard for you. I also understand why you might not want to have a relationship with anybody. But I hope you won't cut me out of your life over what I've just told you.'

'Oh... yeah.' Simon nodded vaguely, obviously having difficulty processing the situation. 'Is this... because you're feeling left behind... boyfriend wise?'

Jaq laughed and wished she hadn't been quite so honest with Simon before.

'I can't deny I've been looking for a boyfriend and I've been on a lot of dates. But at the start, I wasn't thinking of you as a potential boyfriend. Far from it, in fact,' Jaq said, hoping she wasn't saying the wrong thing. 'But lately, I realised I'd stopped going on dates. And when one of my hookups contacted me for a second date, I had no hesitation in turning him down, which surprised me. It made me realise that I'd lost interest in everyone else because I want to spend my time with you.'

'So... you coming round to sleep over?' Simon said, vaguely waving his hand as he grappled with the concept.

'I told myself it was just convenient, or I needed your help. But if I'm honest, I think it was because I was always attracted to you.'

'Oh,' Simon said and looked quite stunned. But whatever he was going to say was cut off by a knocking on the door that led to the stairs. 'The pizza,' Simon said and practically ran to get the delivery.

Hungry as she was, Jaq cursed the delivery guy from showing up at such an inopportune moment. She wasn't in the best frame of mind either, which may have been why she let down her guard and said what she said. Maybe this whole thing had been a mistake. So she just smiled thanks as Simon handed her the box with her pizza. Then he sat down opposite her, on the lip of the concrete block and opened his own box.

He'd gone with a plain pizza, the basics plus olives and sliced tomato. Jaq's hunger had made her go for the maximum toppings: ham, mushrooms, onion, red peppers, pepperoni and artichoke - one of her personal favourites.

Jaq wondered whether Simon might say something now. After all, she'd laid her feeling out for him to see. Would he reciprocate? It didn't look like it.

He was staring at his pizza as if it was the last thing in the world he wanted, and his brow was crinkled in deep and apparently unhappy thought.

'So...' Simon started and took a hold of a slice of pizza, but stopped before lifting it out. He just twisted the crust back and forth. Then he cleared his throat. 'So...'

Whatever he had to say looked like it was difficult, because he was still just twisting that crust, looking nervous.

'I went to therapy because of you,' he said in a rush.

'Shit... I'm sorry,' Jaq said, stunned that she'd caused Simon so much stress.

'No, that came out wrong,' Simon said, finally looking at her, but only for a second before going back to the crust. 'I... you... You made me want to change.'

This was more surprising, and even though she'd lost her appetite, Jaq nibbled on the edge of her pizza so that Simon had the space he needed to say more. She feared that if she said anything, he might clam up.

'You know I've never had a girlfriend,' Simon said in a matter-of-fact tone. 'And because of... what I saw when I was a kid, I was always too scared to get close to a woman in case I... in case I did the same. I didn't want to do what Gregory Black did,' he added in a rush. 'I was just scared I might, and I was scared of being lustful and just... it's hard to explain.'

'That's okay.' Jaq wished she could take back what she'd said, because now it felt like Simon had to explain before he was ready. 'You don't have to tell me anything that makes you uncomfortable.'

'But you made me want to change,' Simon said, doggedly plodding on. 'I was scared of you but also attracted to you, and scared of myself, and the risks and my phobias. But because of you, I went to therapy to try to overcome them.'

'Are you saying you like me?'

'I think so, but I don't know for sure. It's all very confusing for me.'

'I'm glad you told me,' Jaq said, because a thrill of happiness was passing through her despite feeling sorry that she'd sprung this on Simon. 'Don't feel pressured. Despite what you might think, with my relentless search for a boyfriend, I won't rush you.'

Jaq didn't want to push Simon any further. She hadn't expected to hear what he thought of her and what he had been doing. For now, knowing how he felt was good enough. It was time to change the subject, otherwise the skinny man would land up not eating at all.

Jaq was woken at nine by her beeping phone alarm. She jabbed the snooze button for a few more minutes to gather herself. They'd been told not to hurry back to work because of the long hours they'd put in. But Jaq wanted to wrap all the paperwork up, so she'd decided to be back at the station for ten.

She'd stayed the night at Simon's, sleeping on the daybed in the living room. After their talk the previous evening, she was more convinced than ever that he'd bought it for her, despite his initial denial.

Now she lay on her back, hands tucked under her head, staring at the white ceiling, contemplating. She'd been so exhausted and emotionally drained that the whole conversation felt like a dream.

It was amazing what Simon had actually done to be able to be near to her. Or maybe just to cope with her always being around, her demon of doubt said. But no, she'd seen how he dealt with the man who'd hit on her at the pier. Maybe that too had been the protective side guys sometimes showed their girlfriends. Did that explain why he'd stepped in?

Either way, he'd been getting therapy, unspoken and behind the scenes, just so that he could be with her. Or other women, possibly, but she suspected not. Did that mean his feelings were stronger than even he'd admitted to? Or maybe than he knew yet.

'Wow!' she muttered and just then her phone went off again.

It was definitely time to get up. She had enough time to grab a shower and some food and head for the station. Simon's bedroom door was shut, as always. He'd probably left for work hours ago.

Jaq jumped up, stretched up to the ceiling while yawning widely and tried to shake the sleep from her mind. She was bound to need another round of therapy after this case. But time to think about that later. Now she ran for the washing machine, shoved her clothes in and headed for the shower.

It was only when she came out again that she noticed the large cardboard archive box in the middle of the dining room table. It had a nameplate on one end with *Jaq's box* written in elegant letters. The yellow post it stuck below read:

Put your stuff in the box and the box in the entrance cupboard. There's a house key for you stuck to the lid. That way, I won't have your impatient bell ringing.

Simon

P.S. there's milk in the fridge for tea and cereal in the cupboard.

The key taped to the lid on the inside of the box had a red plastic tag with *Jaq's Key* inscribed on it.

'Holy cow,' Jaq murmured. 'That's quite the step forward.'

20

T HE CHATTER OF THE meeting washed over Simon because he was far too preoccupied to pay attention. Unusually, Louise had left the sanctuary of the executive suite to chair the meeting, which should have made him wonder why. But he had bigger problems and doodled in his notebook as he thought.

'Finally,' Louise said and her face took on an unfamiliar eerie smile, 'I have a happy announcement to make. Our dear Sarah is going to have a baby.'

Simon's head snapped up at that and he stared in astonishment at Louise. She was beaming as if she'd achieved some great accomplishment. That was her to a T, always claiming other's work for herself. She was a short, plump woman with plain, mousy brown hair in an unflattering cut. Simon had always wondered how she'd made it to her director position. He suspected it was neither through hard work nor talent.

Now everyone at the table was congratulating Sarah, who was laughing and blushing as she thanked them. Then her eyes caught Simon's, and her mouth pulled into a slight grimace. It warned him that more was to come.

'So now that you've all congratulated Sarah, I'm sure you're wondering who will take over while Sarah is on maternity leave.'

From their reactions it was obvious that most of them hadn't got to wondering about that yet, but everyone turned to look at Simon, who shook his head.

'Sarah and I took a long time thinking about the best way to cover for her and we've decided,' Louise said, the only person who hadn't looked at Simon, 'That we won't be getting in additional cover.'

This surprised Simon so much he sat back, staring at Sarah, whose grimace grew more apologetic.

'As you're all aware, business has been slow lately. Not just for us, but for everybody in the City. So we've decided it would be best if we simply leave the post vacant and divide Sarah's projects up amongst the team. I know that means more work for everyone, but I'm sure we'll cope. Sarah will discuss the details later on. It will be a while before she leaves anyway,' Louise said, stacking her papers. Then she tapped them on the desk to straighten them and sailed out of the room.

'Simon, can I have a word?' Sarah said as everyone stood to leave.

'Sure.'

Simon wanted answers too, so he sat back down.

'Sorry about how things turned out,' Sarah said as the door closed on the last person. 'I don't think Louise had a say in the matter, either. I think this order came from higher up.'

'So... Louise will just be managing all of us?'

'That's the plan. At least you won't have to manage the staff. She had started out with that idea, but I said you wouldn't accept that.'

Simon nodded. That might have pushed him to resign if not for Jaq. Which brought him back to the questions that had been preoccupying him for days.

'It's okay, it can't be helped,' Simon said, waving away something that in the past would have really upset him. 'Can I ask you a personal question?'

'If it's about whether I'll come back, or even whether I'll have a job to come back to, I really don't know.'

'Not that. It's a question about Jaq.'

'Ah!' Sarah said and examined Simon closer than he was comfortable with. 'She told me you two were getting on better.'

'Did she?'

'She seemed really pleased, but you... You've been a bit jittery lately.'

Simon could hardly deny it. But he was a man on a mission, so he was going to push on.

'Is there... what's Jaq's favourite food?'

'That's your personal question?'

Simon nodded, gazing hopefully at Sarah.

'I've been trying to come up with a place to go on a date, but I'm not very good at this kind of thing. Please don't tell anyone about this, not here and especially not Jaq.'

'Don't worry, my lips are sealed. As for Jaq's preferences... She likes novelty. Any new restaurant with a good review will appeal to her. If you can add in a nice ambience or splendid view so much the better.'

Sarah gave a nod and got up to leave. As her hand was reaching for the door, Simon said, 'Which newspaper?'

'What?'

'Which newspaper does she get her reviews from?'

'Oh, that... the Metro sometimes, although I think her favourite food critic writes for the Guardian.'

'Thanks.'

Simon took out his phone and got Siri to call up the Guardian in the search. It surprised him that someone in the police read the Guardian. Then again, he shouldn't make assumptions, and there wasn't anything political about food reviews, he assumed. He couldn't remember ever reading one.

A scan through the food section got him two restaurants with food that had the best chance of being a novelty. Now all that was left was to invite Jaq.

He glanced around the now empty meeting room and through the glass walls at the open plan office. Everyone was absorbed in their own work. Then he flicked on speech to text and paused to consider what he was going to say in his text.

When he was really nervous, he tended to stutter, which gave his phone a hard time and he had to do a bit more editing than usual. He couldn't help thinking how pathetic it was for a grown man to be so anxious about going on a date.

He hoped it wasn't a giant turn off to Jaq. Then again, maybe it would be for the best if it was. He still couldn't decide.

But the text was ready and he jabbed send before he could chicken out.

If you're not busy, would you like to go to dinner this Friday?

210

MARINA PACHECO

He stared at the message in disbelief. He'd actually had the nerve to send it. His hand shook all the more when the message showed as read. He held his breath, but nothing happened.

Still he waited, staring at the screen, trying to guess what Jaq was thinking. Was she just too busy to answer? Was she offended and trying to think of a way to get him to back off? Would she reply at all?

Sure, where do you want to go?

The message pinged onto his screen like a miracle and relief flooded over Simon. That was rapidly followed by the horrified realisation that he had actually asked a woman out on a date.

Vietnamese in Crystal Palace or Peruvian in Peckham? He texted back, including the links with the two reviews.

It took a while to get a reply, presumably because Jaq was reading the reviews.

Let's go Peruvian — 7pm? She finally texted.

Simon let go of his breath. He hadn't realised he'd gone back to holding it. Then his whole body turned to jelly. He'd done it. He'd actually gone and done it.

Jaq was thrilled that Simon had taken the initiative and invited her out. Their last encounter had made her decide to back off and put him under less pressure. So the text had come as a pleasant surprise.

Now she'd done her best to dress for a date and not look like a detective. This meant letting her hair down, wearing a dress and a bit of makeup. Hopefully she looked pretty, but not over the top, she thought as she slowed down to examine herself in the dark glass of a bank window. Simple but elegant, she decided, and sufficient for a restaurant that the critic had described as homey.

Simon was already outside, pacing back and forth at the entrance, in full view of a CCTV camera. Since it was Peckham High Street, there were dozens of cameras, so it wasn't necessarily deliberate. Jaq checked her watch. It was five to seven.

'I hope I didn't keep you waiting,' she said as she approached.

Simon's face lit up with a smile that slightly faltered as a flicker of fear crossed it.

Jaq reached out to take Simon's hand and gave it a brief squeeze before letting go, noting the tremor as she did. So he was nervous, but hiding it quite well.

'Shall we go in?'

'Yes,' Simon said, and he sounded a bit breathless.

But he also looked happier than Jaq had seen before, which made her feel good, too. A very young waitress showed them to a table by the window, looking out onto the High Street. It was lit by the golden glow of a slowly setting sun, and Jaq smiled at her appreciatively. It felt like they were getting the best table in this narrow little restaurant with its orange painted walls and cactus decorations.

'I'll be right back with the menus,' the waitress said and hurried away.

'I think she fancies you,' Jaq said with a grin as she sat down opposite Simon.

'What?' he said, looking surprised.

'You're good looking,' Jaq said with a laugh. 'Didn't you know that? It's what first attracted me to you, and obviously what the waitress likes too, and from what Sarah's told me, all the women in your office.' Simon blushed, which made Jaq laugh. 'Did nobody ever tell you this?'

'It may have been mentioned before. I didn't believe them. But you look very nice today, too.'

'Thank you. I haven't forgotten that you said I was attractive when we were in Brighton. That was my first clue that you weren't entirely indifferent to me.'

'It feels like a long time ago.'

'Another world. So much has happened since. Oh, including my sister having her baby. I now have a very cute niece.'

'Congratulations,' Simon said with a slight smile that made it feel like he really meant it.

Or perhaps it was simply politeness, nothing more. But it made Jaq wonder whether she could or ever would introduce Simon to the rest of her family. Her aunt had already told her mother all about the tall, dark and handsome stranger Jaq had brought to Brighton. Her words, of course. This had got her some teasing from the whole family and a more thorough interrogation from her mother. But it was too soon to bring that sort of thing up with Simon.

'How was your day?'

'Fine,' Simon said, more monosyllabic than usual. He knew it too because it looked like he was trying to come up with something more to say. 'Sarah won't get a stand in when she goes on leave.'

'And you?'

'I won't be acting up. We'll all just be taking on more work.'

'Typical! We have the same sort of crap to deal with in the force. It's always more work and shrinking budgets. Just for once, I wish they'd give us more money and recruit more. My unit's woefully understaffed.'

'Is it?'

Jaq waved her hand to dismiss the topic.

'It makes me too angry, and that's not why we came out today. Let's not discuss politics.'

'And work in general,' Simon murmured.

'That too,' Jaq agreed and made room so the waitress could deposit their plates. Two very impressive servings of seafood ceviche smothered in tiger's milk. 'Wow, this looks great.'

Simon nodded but looked more worried about the food that had been served to them in a glass usually reserved for ice cream sundaes as he picked up his fork and prodded a dangling octopus leg.

'It's delicious,' Jaq said after she'd tasted a chunk of fish smothered in the sauce. 'Tart but oh so moreish.'

'Okay,' Simon said and took a first hesitant mouthful, aiming for a shrimp.

Jaq left him to it and took a sip of the tequila based cocktail she'd opted for. When she was savouring food she tended to let conversation drop. This was perfect, and just what she'd needed to finish what had been a quiet week.

Following on from the harrowing child murder case, Jaq had taken the week off work. The entire team needed the time to destress and get over the case. Jaq even took the counselling the team was offered.

It was often seen as a matter of pride to say you didn't need it. Tough detectives toughing it out. Sometimes, she also wondered whether the counselling helped or made it worse, getting you to linger over horrific experiences that were best forgotten.

In the end, she got the counselling. The woman who saw her was reassuringly professional and unemotional. It was exactly what Jaq needed. If she'd shown too much sympathy, Jaq might have burst into tears. Darren had said the same when he got back to the office after his session.

Thinking about the counselling made her look back up at Simon. How shit must his life have been to need years of counselling. It wasn't a question she was going to ask. The little bits that he said about his past, and the way he led his life, spoke of a man who still had a hell of a lot of hangups. Too many hangups.

When she'd first got to know him, Jaq had been suspicious of Simon and his past. A boyfriend with a record was undesirable, to say the least. Now, that hardly bothered her, but his emotional damage had become a preoccupation.

She'd met many traumatised victims of crime, some a once off, some people who'd endured years of violence or psychological abuse. It had scarred them deeply and very few were able to simply move on.

Superficially, Simon had. When it came to work, or day to day living, he seemed to be doing fine. Relationships, on the other hand, were so frightening to him that he'd never had one until now. She wasn't sure she was ready or willing to deal with that kind of damage.

'That was great.' Jaq pushed aside her concerns as she finished the last of the ceviche and mopped up the sauce with a fragment of bread. 'It looks like you enjoyed it too,' she said, noting that Simon had also finished the entire serving for a change. 'Fancy desert?'

'Sure,' Simon said. 'So... are you glad you came?'

'Very glad. This Peruvian food is amazing, and very different. I'm glad to have discovered it, especially as we came together.'

Simon smiled. Now he looked more confident and relaxed.

'I think I'll have the three milks pudding.'

'That looks really sweet,' Jaq said, reading the ingredients, 'caramel and condensed milk plus cream. I think I'll go for something less loaded with sugar. I didn't realise you had such a sweet tooth. We should have had an ice cream in Brighton, too.'

'I didn't get any sweets growing up, so maybe I'm overcompensating now,' Simon said, as if referring to a perfectly normal childhood perhaps with overly health conscious parents.

'I suppose so. Thinking back, I remember that you also ate all the mango and sticky rice from the Thai.'

'That was really good.'

Jaq nodded and wondered whether that was also why Simon had opted for the non-alcoholic fruit juice rather than the cocktail. Was it merely because he liked sweets? Or was it because he was worried about losing control if he got drunk?

'That was nice,' Jaq said as they walked back to the train station past the night time crowds that had built up, ready to party the night away. 'Do you fancy holding hands?'

Simon looked down at her, surprised.

'No pressure. If you aren't ready for it, don't worry.'

Simon nodded, then held his hand out, palm up. There was only a very slight tremor in the gesture. Jaq smiled up at him and placed her hand over his, curling her fingers around his palm. He only hesitated a fraction of a second before doing the same.

The pressure of Simon's warm hand was so nice and so distracting that the hubbub of the passers buy faded from Jaq's awareness. It felt like it was only the two of them, strolling along like lovers. It was such a tiny gesture and yet felt more intimate than anything Jaq had ever experienced before.

Yeah, this had to be love. The real deal, the thing she had never felt with any of those easy guys, the one-night stands, the high earners, the athletes, the guys who were willing to kiss and have sex on the first date. How could this be possible?

The station came into view far too soon for Jaq and she regretted they had to let go of each other to get through the ticket barriers. Then they were in the rather full foyer that led to the stairs for the different platforms.

'I guess this is where we say goodbye,' Jaq said sadly as she pulled Simon into a quieter corner, out of the flow of commuters.

She was going west, Simon was heading east.

'Yeah, I guess so. Text me when you get home.'

'I will. You do the same.'

'Me?'

'Of course, or do you think I won't worry about my boyfriend?' Jaq said, feeling daring as she took hold of both of Simon's hands.

They were standing so close to each other that she could feel his body heat.

'Would you be okay with a farewell kiss?'

Simon leaned away and a look of panic flickered across his face, but then he gave a slight nod.

Jaq leaned forward, raising her head as the world around her receded again, and all she could see was Simon's cheek. She gave him a light peck before she leaned back, looking him in the eye and kissed him on the lips. Soft, warm lips she couldn't resist. She kissed him once, and then again, longer. Her tongue pushed forward, running along the gap between his unyielding lips.

'Stop!' Simon said and pushed her away.

'Simon, I'm sorry. Did I go too far?' Jaq was horrified by how pale he'd turned, and she reached for his hand.

'I can't do this,' Simon said in a strangled voice, tears starting to his eyes as he pulled his hand away. 'I really can't do this!' Then he turned and ran.

'Simon!' Jaq shouted, feeling stupid.

How could she have been so impatient? What had she done now? She had to apologise.

Jaq hurried up the stairs, looking for Simon. Then she froze. He was leaning against the far wall, propping himself up by his hands, throwing up. He looked miserable and she feared if she tried to go to his aid, he'd feel worse.

Jaq backed away and headed for her platform. She dropped onto one of the metal benches and stared out into the night. She'd ruined what could have been a wonderful evening.

Sure, Simon was tenser than usual, but that was because it was a first for him. If they'd parted on good terms, he'd have been able to see that everything was okay and they'd probably have kept inching towards a relationship.

But now? Now he'd had an extremely negative reaction to such a simple little thing. Just a kiss. But he was so freaked out that she worried it had set their relationship right back.

21

'I T'S HARD TO BELIEVE summer is nearly over,' Jaq said as she clinked a bottle of beer against Darren's offered one.

She was slouched in one of his plastic garden chairs at his annual BBQ. Several excitable kids were chasing each other while knots of adults stood about chatting. Darren's wife toiled over a smoky fire at the far end of the garden, expertly turning pork sausages and chicken thighs, and now and then handing one to an expectant guest.

'August bank holiday, when it feels like the summer will never end, but you know it's dwindling fast.'

Darren leaned back in his chair and took a deep, satisfying swig of lager.

'Mmm.'

'I thought I might actually see you here with a man this year.'

'Simon?'

'You were spending a lot of time with him.'

'I haven't seen him or heard from him in two weeks.'

Darren actually looked surprised, which Jaq counted as a win. Usually she couldn't slip anything past this veteran detective, be it work related or about her private life.

Jaq waited for a question, but Darren wasn't the type to pry. Aside from that, he was an excellent interrogator who left the other person to fill in the silence.

Since Jaq had been driving herself crazy trying to work out where she went next with Simon, she said, 'I've been trying to decide whether it's better to just leave him be, or reach out to him again. We didn't exactly part on the best of terms.'

'Oh yeah?'

'I kissed him and he freaked out.'

'Consensual?'

'Mostly,' Jaq said, squirming. 'He agreed to a kiss, but it may have been more intense than he was expecting. I shouldn't have done it. But his reaction was also extreme.'

Darren nodded.

'I looked into him after you started going to his. I was worried because of his background.'

'He was right about that. A cloud of suspicion will always hang over him.'

'Did you know that his father didn't only use him to lure women in, he also forced the kid to watch as he raped and murdered the women?'

'Yeah, I had a look at his files, too.' That information had made Jaq feel sick in itself. Now she feared she must have triggered a traumatic memory with her kiss. 'That bastard father.'

'Gregory Black told his kid he was an accomplice because he helped lure the women in and then saw everything,' Darren said, gazing out across the bright green lawn and the cheerful guests. 'And our legal system pretty much agreed. Although with Simon's background, it was probably better for him and society that he was eased into normal life rather than just released into it.'

'I agree. They did a pretty good job with whatever therapy they gave him. It's surprising really that he turned out as normal as he did.'

'Yeah.' Darren paused, waiting for the romping kids to move out of earshot, barked at by the excitable family dog. 'According to the info I got, your man suffers from extreme anxiety and depression. He was a bundle of terrified nerves at the young offenders' institution. Probably because his father put the fear of God into him about what would happen to him in prison, so he didn't mingle there either.'

'Probably best that he didn't, as he told me himself. He'd just have ended up hanging out with the wrong crowd.'

'And he got lucky because one of those do-gooder arts charities picked up on the fact that he draws really well. He landed up getting three years of intensive art lessons along with all his therapy while he was locked up and being evaluated. After it was determined that he wouldn't be a threat to society, the charity got him into art college, but he was closely supervised all the way along. After that, much to everybody's surprise, he got a job at that ad agency and has been living a respectable life ever since.'

'He even bought himself a flat.'

'Bought and fully paid for,' Darren said, giving Jaq a smug smile, because he knew that was going to surprise her.

'Seriously, it's paid off? How? I mean, his job isn't even management. The pay can't be that good, even if he barely spends any money, which I can believe because, well, who is he going to spend it on? That flat couldn't have been cheap.'

'He's got a side gig.'

'He never mentioned it to me.'

'He's not used to making conversation, is he? But I got curious when I saw his place. My Brenda is mad keen on interior decorating.'

'You don't need to tell me that.'

Jaq was all too familiar with Brenda's obsession that led to an overly done up house and piles of interior magazines in the loo.

'So I could tell at a glance that Simon's house is full of good quality stuff, expensive.'

'And a good copper knows to always follow the money. If you hadn't mentioned the side gig, I might have guessed an inheritance. Gregory Black owned his house too, didn't he?'

'That was my first guess. But it turns out Simon donated all the money from his father's estate to a women's refuge.'

'Ah... I can understand why.' Jaq couldn't imagine living off money made by a serial killer, even if your circumstances were dire. 'So, where does he make his money?'

'He sells those paintings of his.'

'The big sky paintings?'

'At ten grand a pop.'

'Holy shit! Ten thousand pounds for one painting?' Jaq reached for the remains of a sausage in a bun and took a bite.

'And he sells more or less one a month.'

'That's a lot of money. I guess more people than I realised could use some sky therapy.'

'Huh?'

'Nothing.' Jaq waved dismissal, popped the rest of the bun into her mouth and chewed meditatively. 'So he's actually doing okay for himself. Except in one area. He has no friends.'

'He probably doesn't have the skill set for it. Making friends is something you learn when you're a kid. It probably did him good to have you force your way into his life. It's the only way he's ever going to make friends, and most people aren't willing to make the effort.'

Jaq gave a cynical laugh.

'My motives weren't exactly pure.'

'Maybe not, but he did you some good too, you know?'

'He did?' Jaq was so surprised her hand froze halfway towards conveying a bottle of lager to her lips.

'You've become a more compassionate cop, which is good. And on a personal note, you've been more relaxed, happier, and just that little bit more positive. It's done you good to have a boyfriend.'

'Now wait a moment. We were super platonic. I mean, super, super platonic. Nothing happened.'

'But you felt better about yourself, and coped with our cases better too, didn't you?'

Jaq hadn't even considered it, but looking back, she had to admit Darren was right.

'Shit!'

'So what are you going to do about it now?' Darren asked, and it sounded like a challenge.

Simon stood in front of his canvas. He'd pulled the
curtain in his bedroom right back so that he had a clear
view of the sky. It wasn't particularly interesting today,
just some thin threads of fluffy white lines against
a washed out blue. It was okay. He usually painted
from photos and those he took on his phone, snapping
anything that made him feel relaxed or that might look
good on a gigantic canvas. The large canvas was a must.
It was the only way to do justice to the majesty of the
sky and the clouds.

His heart wasn't in it today though, and he removed
the top canvas and gazed at the one below. It was a
picture of Jaq, fast asleep on the daybed. He hardly
ever painted people except for work, but he couldn't
stop working on this one. As his brush traced along the
canvas, he wondered about Jaq.

The kiss had come as a shock and he'd reacted on
instinct, running and hiding. But after he'd got over his
panic, the questions started piling in. Did she really like
him? She's said as much, but was it true?

That was what a kiss meant, didn't it? Did it? People
seemed quite casual about kisses in the workplace. But
they were to the cheek, never on the lips.

His mind kept going back to that moment and the
same push pull of emotions he got whenever he touched
anyone, but especially women. He'd been told by Dr
Nobel that touch was a basic human need. Children that
were never given love, and had never been held, had died of

sadness. He understood that. But touch was hard for him because it brought terrible memories with it.

Except for two. The day Jaq had taken his hand on the roof and the kiss. Nauseated as he was, he couldn't block it from his memory and sometimes all that came to mind was the warmth of her lips and the trembling softness of her tongue as it pressed against his mouth. Then he desperately wanted her to kiss him again.

He'd waited for her, too. He was certain she'd ignore everything he'd said and turn up with a takeaway, breezing in like nothing had happened. But it was a month since the night of the kiss and there was no sign of Jaq. She hadn't returned his key either, and he clung onto that as a sign of hope, but it was a dwindling one.

His last words to her had been to leave him alone. It looked like she was going to follow his order. A whole month! He'd never felt lonelier or more alone in his life.

At least he'd learned one thing from this separation. He didn't want to lose Jaq. Since he was the one who'd told her to stay away, it was up to him to make the first move, since she'd clearly decided she had to accept his screamed demand.

For the hundredth time, he picked up his phone and looked at the text he'd written weeks ago. His finger hovered over the send button, trembling. What if she never answered?

'Coward,' he muttered and stabbed the button. It was gone with a muted ping.

Are you alright?

Funny how he'd agonised over those three words, worried that they said too much, didn't say enough, were too vague, even though he'd written and rewritten the damn thing, sometimes making it longer, sometimes shorter.

His hand was shaking harder now as he held the phone, staring at the little sent speech bubble. Would she reply?

Read. Jaq had read the text. Now what? He couldn't look away. What if she left him on read? What then? Was that when he'd have to accept that he'd messed up his one chance at friendship or more?

Shouldn't I be asking you that?

The ping of the arriving message made him jump, and he had to read the little glowing bubble three times before he could believe it. She'd answered him, and she'd asked a question. So now he had an excuse to text her again.

I'm fine. It wasn't enough, but his mind was panicked, excited, blank. *I miss you.*

Simon pressed send before he had time to regret and then cursed himself. It was too much. Too clingy.

Are you at home?

It's the weekend, of course I'm home.

Every message left him breathlessly anxious, worried that one wrong word would end it all, desperate not to make a mistake, and yet, the last message, that was stupid.

Don't go anywhere, Jaq messaged. *I'm coming.*

Simon blinked at the phone. Typical Jaq, she was a woman of action. Thank God.

22

— • —

IT TOOK SO BLOODY long to get to Simon's that Jaq was cursing with impatience. Then, even though she'd phoned her order in for the takeaway, and needed an hour to get across London, the damn food wasn't ready when she arrived.

Jaq checked her phone, the same way she'd done a hundred times on the journey over. Simon hadn't replied. Hopefully, it was because he was patiently waiting at home.

Finally, the food was done and Jaq snatched the bag out of the man's hands and ran all the way to Simon's taking the stairs two at a time so she was breathless and had to fold over double when she reached the top floor to recover.

The light directly above Simon's door was on. That gave Jaq a frisson of pleasure. Simon was waiting for her.

Despite that, she rang the doorbell and tried to still the butterflies in her stomach as she waited. The camera light came on, so she did the usual of holding the takeaway up and smiled. She hoped she didn't look too cheesy.

'Don't you have your key?' Simon asked as he opened the door.

'Of course I do, but considering how we parted last time and how long it's been...' Jaq shrugged. No need to say

more, especially when Simon looked on edge. It was up to
her to get him to relax. 'I brought kebabs. It's my kind of
comfort food and also because I suspected you'd need it.
You've lost weight again.'

The flicker of a smile twitched Simon's lips and he
stepped back, waving an arm for her to enter. Jaq sighed
with relief and grinned at him as she sailed inside.

'Do you like kebabs? I should have asked before I
bought it. I went with the least offensive flavours I could
think of, though.'

'Least offensive?' Simon said, heading for the kitchen to
take down two of his largest plates.

'Chicken rather than lamb and with the chilli sauce on
the side.'

Jaq felt like she was rambling. She was frustrated with
herself but couldn't think of anything else to say. Were
they just going to pretend that nothing happened at
Peckham Station?

'I like both chicken and lamb kebabs,' Simon said,
handed Jaq a glass for her beer, put one down for himself
and sat down, looking expectantly up at Jaq.

Man, this was difficult. Jaq hadn't felt this nervous since
the first time she'd phoned her crush to go to a school
dance. She tipped her kebab onto the plate, then poured
half the chilli sauce over it, and watched as Simon did the
same.

'I'm sorry about... what I did last time.'

Jaq felt Simon needed an apology but also worried that
he might not take well to being reminded. His hand gave
a tremor, and he put the kebab down and slid both hands
onto his lap. It was what he always did to hide his nerves.
Maybe she should have waited before saying anything.

Maybe she shouldn't have brought the subject up at all. No, it was hanging over them, making things awkward.

'I've been thinking about it,' Simon said in a strained voice. 'I overreacted.'

'You acted on instinct against something that scared you. There's no need for you to apologise.'

'The thing is... as you know, I find it very difficult to touch people. Especially women,' Simon said, looking up. 'I thought I'd prepared myself, and that I was ready. But at that moment,' Simon stopped, shaking his head.

His agonised expression was tough to face.

'It's okay. We can take it easy, be friends and—'

'No!' Simon surprised Jaq with the vehemence in his voice. 'I don't want to be relegated to friend status. I want... I'm still seeing my therapist. She said I can get over my phobia as long as I really want to.'

'Do you want to?' Jaq said partly to help Simon say more and also because she really wanted to know.

'I hadn't seen her in a while. I'd reached a stage in my life I felt okay with. Work was fine and nothing was changing. So I stopped going. But now... now I have something really important to work on.'

Being called really important reassured Jaq, and she felt herself relaxing.

'Okay, let's take it slow and be guided by your therapist. How does that sound?'

'Good,' Simon said and finally gave Jaq a half decent smile. 'I have something to show you,' he said as he shot to his feet.

'Really? Here?'

'Yeah, come on.'

Simon hurried to his room, leaving the door open for her to follow. That was a first. Jaq's mind seethed with speculation. What on earth could it be that meant Simon was inviting her into his inner sanctum? Easy girl, she warned herself, don't get carried away.

'Oh, your easel, I should have realised it was here,' Jaq said, following Simon, who'd made his way to the large window with the same gauzy curtains as in the sitting room. Simon had set the easel up so that he'd have a good view of the sky, much the same as when it had been in the living room.

'I've been painting something different,' Simon said and waved his hand at the gigantic canvas.

'Wow,' Jaq breathed.

The top of the picture was an almost cloud like representation of the curtain, billowing inwards, golden light playing on it and the wall behind, but the bottom third was the olive green daybed with a woman curled up on it, wrapped in a soft green fleece that melded into the colours of the sofa, her hair falling across her face obscuring her features.

'It's me!'

'I was going through the security footage when I saw this image and I couldn't resist. I hope you don't mind.'

'I'm really flattered, actually. Nobody has ever painted me before, and on such an enormous canvas. You're not going to sell this one, are you?'

Simon looked disconcerted for a second and shook his head. 'How did you know?'

'Darren, you remember the D.I. I work with, has a habit of checking out all my boyfriends. He told me you sell your work.'

Jaq couldn't take her eyes off the painting. It was really beautiful. She had a hard time reconciling that beauty with her own image of herself. Then Simon's fingers brushed along the side of her hand and she looked down. He looked like he wanted to hold her hand, so she opened it and turned it upwards invitingly.

'Don't leave me, Jaq,' Simon said, as he took hold of her hand and gave it a squeeze.

'I'm not going anywhere,' Jaq said, smiling up at him.

Simon gazed at her, happiness, nerves and something that looked like growing determination chased across his face. His grip on her hand tightened as he leaned down and gave Jaq a peck on the lips.

'I'll work at getting better,' he murmured.

Then as if the first kiss had given him courage he leaned in for a longer, softer kiss and Jaq put her arm gently around his waist. 'Together, we'll be able to overcome everything.'

GET MY SHORT STORY COLLECTION SHORTIES FOR FREE!

Sign up for my no-spam newsletter that only goes out when there is a new book or freebie available and get my collection of short stories for free, at: https://substack.com/@marinapacheco

Find out more about me and all my books: www.marinapacheco.me

ALSO BY

Get all my books here:

MEDIEVAL HISTORICAL FICTION ePub, paperback and hardback
Fraternity of Brothers, *Life of Galen, Book 1* – Cast out for a crime committed against him, his future looks bleak. Until an unexpected visitor gives him hope for justice. A fight for acceptance, absolution and friendship in Anglo-Saxon England.
Comfort of Home, *Life of Galen, Book 2* – Proven innocent, he's returned from exile. Can he recover all that he lost? A tale of friendship and return to a family he thought he'd lost, set in Anglo-Saxon England.
Kindness of Strangers, *Life of Galen, Book 3* – Trapped in a land plagued by vikings, can one small miracle be all they need to survive? A tale of miracles, betrayal and friendship while under viking siege.
The King's Hall, *Life of Galen, Book 4* – As if

being commissioned to create a book to turn back the Apocalypse isn't enough, intrigue and romance threaten to destroy everything he's come to rely upon. Friendship, love and intrigue at the court of King Aethelred the Unready.

Restless Sea, *Life of Galen, Book 5* – Just when they thought they could go home, they're thrust into an adventure at sea. A journey that tests the bonds of friendship.

Friend of My Enemy, *Life of Galen, Book 6* – Captured by an implacable enemy, their future looks bleak. Will escape even be possible?

Road to Rome, *Life of Galen, Book 7* — A journey across a turbulent continent. Will Galen find the answers he seeks?

Eternal City, *Life of Galen, Book 8* — Galen and Alcuin delve into the secrets of the corrupt and decaying city of Medieval Rome.

AUDIOBOOKS narrated by Jacob Daniels
Fraternity of Brothers, *Life of Galen, Book 1*
Comfort of Home, *Life of Galen, Book 2*
Kindness of Strangers, *Life of Galen, Book 3*
The King's Hall, *Life of Galen, Book 4*
    Restless Sea, *Life of Galen, Book 5*

HISTORICAL ROMANCE: ePub, paperback, hardback and audiobooks with AI narration
Sanctuary, *a sweet Medieval mystery* – He needs shelter.

She wants a way out. Will his brave move to protect risk both their hearts? An optimistic tale of redemption with heart-warming characters and feel-good thrills.

The Duke's Heart, *a sweet Victorian romance* – His body may be weak, but his dreams know no bounds. Will she be the answer to his prayers? A disabled duke, a strong and determined woman and a slow-building relationship.

Duchess in Flight, *a swashbuckling romance* – She's on the run from a deadly enemy. He lives in the shadows of truth. When their lives merge, will their battle for survival lead to love? A reluctant hero, a woman and her children in distress, a chase to the death.

What the Pauper Did, *a body swap mystery romance* – How do you define yourself? Is it through your appearance, your memories or your soul? Intrigue, murder and romance in an alternate Lisbon of 1770.

CONTEMPORARY ROMANCE ePub, paperback, hardback and audiobooks with AI narration

Scent of Love – Can two polar opposite perfumers overcome their differences and create a unique blend all of their own? Love, intrigue and clashing values in the perfume houses of Lisbon.

Sky Therapy — A detective and the son of a serial killer. Is it safest to stay apart, or will they risk everything for love?

Terapia Celeste — My first novel (Sky Therapy) to be translated into Brazilian Portuguese.

SCIENCE FICTION/ FANTASY ePub and paperback
City of Night, *Eternal City, Book 1* – World-threatening danger, a female demonologist, an unwitting apprentice, a city in a single tower, a satisfying ending.

SHORT STORIES: ePub, paperback, and AI narration
Living, Loving, Longing, Lisbon, Vol 1 & Vol 2 – A collection of short stories inspired by the city of Lisbon, written by people from around the world who live in, visited or love Lisbon.
Loves of Lisbon – A Christmas advent calendar of 24 short, sweet romances of the intertwining lives of the residents of Lisbon.

FREEBIES: ePub and AI narration
Shorties – My shortest works: futuristic, contemporary and historical available for free when you sign up to my newsletter.

ABOUT AUTHOR

Marina Pacheco a binge writer of historical fiction, sweet romance, sci-fi and fantasy novels as well as short stories. She writes easy reading, feel-good novels that are perfect for a commute or to curl up with on a rainy day. She currently lives on the coast just outside Lisbon, after stints in London, Johannesburg, and Bangkok, which all sounds more glamorous than it actually was. Her ambition is to publish 100 books. This is taking considerably longer than she'd anticipated!

You can find out more about Marina Pacheco's work, and download several freebies, on her website: https://marinapacheco.me
Website: https://marinapacheco.me
 Sign up to Marina's newsletter via her website or on Substack to keep up to date on all her writing activities, get early previews of covers and first chapters, short stories and freebies.
Follow me on substack:
https://substack.com/@marinapacheco
email: hi@marinapacheco.me